Touching Rune
Second Chance Bc

NYT & USA
Bestselling Author

S E SMITH

Touching
RUNE

SECOND CHANCE SERIES BOOK TWO

By S.E. Smith

Acknowledgments

I would like to thank my husband Steve for believing in me and being proud enough of me to give me the courage to follow my dream. I would also like to give a special thank you to my sister and best friend Linda, who not only encouraged me to write but who also read the manuscript. Also to my other friends who believe in me: Julie, Jackie, Lisa, Sally, Elizabeth (Beth) and Narelle. The girls that keep me going!

—S.E. Smith

Montana Publishing
Paranormal Romance
TOUCHING RUNE: SECOND CHANCE BOOK 2
Copyright © 2013 by S.E. Smith
First E-Book Published December 2013
Cover Design by Melody Simmons
ALL RIGHTS RESERVED: This literary work may not be reproduced or transmitted in any form or by any means, including electronic or photographic reproduction, in whole or in part, without express written permission from the author.

All characters, places, and events in this book are fictitious or have been used fictitiously, and are not to be construed as real. Any resemblance to actual persons living or dead, actual events, locales, or organizations are strictly coincidental.

Summary: Rune was able to continue to protect the orphans of St. Agnes Home after she died by becoming a statue on the grounds, but now she has been sold, and she's about to change the lives of the men who bought her.

ISBN: 978-1-942562-56-6 (paperback)
ISBN: 978-1-942562-17-7 (eBook)

Published in the United States by Montana Publishing.

{1. Paranormal Romance – Fiction. 2. Paranormal – Fiction. 3. Romance – Fiction.}

www.montanapublishinghouse.com

Synopsis

Rune August embraces her life in New York City in 1894. She has lived again and again through many different time periods, but has never found tranquility until she walked into St. Agnes Home for Orphans. In her heart, she believes she has found a place she can call home. She will do everything she can to give the children in the orphanage a better life.

When a developer sets his sights on the property she and the children call home, she doesn't hesitate to fight back - and win. But that win comes at a terrible price... her life... casting her once again into the shadows.

Refusing to leave the children unprotected, she watches over and protects them in a different form... as the beloved statue in their center garden. But her time as the children's guardian angel draws to a close when the orphanage is renovated. Rune finds herself packed away and sold. Her new home is now far away from the familiar streets of New York and the children she loves.

Sergei Vasiliev and his best friend and bodyguard, Dimitri Mihailov, run one of the most powerful computer software development companies in the world. Both men carry deep scars from their life on the streets and from living in the world of the ultra-rich. Sergei knows men want him for his power and women want him for his money. Dimitri knows that some men and women would do anything to gain the secrets their company is developing.

Their lives change when Sergei purchases a statue for their home outside of Moscow. There is something about the statue of the young woman that touches an unexpected need deep inside both of them.

An impulsive purchase and a simple wish will change their lives forever. For anyone who touches Rune learns that love and hope are what makes the world a better place. Can she warm the hearts of two bitter, scarred men before the last petal falls from the Christmas rose that grows in the garden that has become her new home or will she be forever frozen, destined to only love them from afar?

Contents

Chapter 1

New York City, St. Agnes Orphanage 1894

"Rune, look at me!" Mary Katherine cried out as she twirled around in the new dress that Sister Helen had made for her. "Don't I look beautiful? Do you think the Wrights will choose me?"

Rune grinned as the excited six year twirled around in a circle so her dress would fly out around her. Sister Mary stood to the side smiling serenely. Neither one of them let on that the faded dress had seen better days or had been passed down time and time again. To both of them, Mary Katherine looked beautiful with her shiny brown curls and rosy cheeks.

"I think the last thing you need is a bouquet of flowers to give Mrs. Wright," Rune said as she pulled the left over flowers she had tucked away for just this occasion. "I bet she would love them as much as she'll love you."

Mary Katherine gasped and ran over to give Rune a huge hug before she carefully took the small offering. Her eyes shone with excitement as she stared into Rune's warm brown eyes. A small dimple formed as she smiled up at Rune.

"Oh thank you, Rune," Mary Katherine whispered. "I'll take very good care of them until they come."

"It is a good thing that won't be long," Sister Anna said sternly from behind Mary Katherine. "Come along, Mary Katherine. The Wrights are here to see you now."

Rune leaned down and hugged the delicate little girl. "Remember to smile and be polite," she whispered. "They are going to love you as much as I do."

"I love you too, Rune," Mary Katherine whispered before she gave Rune a quick kiss on her cheek.

"Go shine for them, rosebud," Rune whispered back as she watched Mary Katherine follow Sister Anna into the orphanage.

Sister Mary walked over to where Rune stood watching the departing figures. She brushed a strand of long dark brown hair back behind Rune's ear that had fallen loose. She studied the face of the young woman who had appeared out of nowhere five years before when they desperately needed help.

A serious outbreak of Whooping Cough had struck the orphanage. The four Sisters of St. Agnes had been unable to handle the almost thirty children who contracted it. Rune had walked in and taken over when Sister Helen and Mother Magdalene came down sick as well. She had been a part of their small family ever since.

"Do you think they'll adopt her?" Rune asked in a soft, worried voice.

"Only God knows, child," Sister Mary said. "My goodness, what happened to your wrist?"

Rune looked down at her wrist in surprise. She started to pull the sleeve of her blouse back over it, but Sister Mary reached down and gently gripped her hand so she could take a closer look at the dark bruises that marred the delicate skin.

"It's nothing," Rune started to say but Sister Mary refused to release her right wrist.

"Who did this to you?" Sister Mary asked in concern. "Was it that dreadful Mr. Randolph?"

"Sister Mary," Rune sighed. "He came to see me over in the market. I took care of him. There is nothing to worry about."

"What did he want?" Sister Mary demanded. "Was it about the orphanage again? The church will not sell him the property. We have a written agreement from the Archbishop himself that as long as there are children living here that it will remain open."

"I told him that," Rune replied, looking around the garden that she had created for the children. "He... wanted me to convince you that you needed to change the Archbishop's mind or he would have to take matters into his own hands."

"You need to tell Mother Magdalene. She needs to know he threatened you," Sister Mary insisted. "What else did he say?"

Rune blushed and lowered her head. She couldn't tell the Sisters what else Walter Randolph said. She had become livid at his crude comments and she had let him know she would not let him talk to her in such a manner. She brushed her long braid over her shoulder and shrugged instead of answering Sister Mary.

"He just wanted me to convince Mother Magdalene to talk to the Archbishop," she mumbled.

Sister Mary's lips tightened as she looked at the lovely young woman standing in front of her. She could see the flush on her cheeks and the anger in her eyes as she looked at the ground. She reached out and touched Rune's cheek and smiled in understanding.

"You are a very lovely young woman, Rune," Sister Mary said. "You have a heart of gold and you have given that gold to not only the children who live here but to the Sisters of St. Agnes. I just want you to know that we are here for you as well."

Rune lifted her head and gazed at Sister Mary with a look of determination in her eyes. "You… all of you… are the family I lost," Rune whispered. "I won't let anything happen to you. I'll protect you and the children, no matter what Randolph threatens to do."

"You are part of our family as well, Rune," Sister Mary said. "Never doubt that."

Rune smiled and was about to reply when suddenly the center courtyard garden was overflowing with excited children. Mary Katherine came running as fast as her legs could move. She had a huge grin on her face.

"Rune! I've got a family," she called out as she threw herself into Rune's open arms. "I have a mommy and daddy."

"And they have a beautiful daughter," Rune laughed as she swung Mary Katherine around in a circle before setting her down and smiling at the young couple walking toward her.

"I believe these came from you," the young woman said with a smile as she lifted the small bouquet of flowers. "Thank you."

Rune smiled back. "No, thank you," she responded as the other children gathered around to wish Mary Katherine goodbye.

Rune watched with a combination of happiness and sadness. She had dreamed a long time ago about having a family, but it was not meant to be. Instead, she accepted the children and Sisters into her heart and let them fill her life with joy.

She looked around the cheerful garden that she had worked hard on. Brilliant flowers bloomed everywhere. They reminded her of the children; each different, delicate yet colorful.

Yes, I will do everything in my power to protect them, she thought as love swelled inside her. *This is what I was meant to do.*

Chapter 2

Rune turned the corner and held her breath as she pressed her back against the cold brick and mortar building. Walter Randolph and his men were looking for her. She cursed under her breath. Ruby had warned her as she gathered the last of her flowers that had not sold for the day. Ruby, who sold scented soap beside her, had told her that she would take care of everything and have her brother drop it off at the orphanage later that evening.

Rune had barely had time to whisper her thanks before one of Randolph's men spotted her. Hiking her long skirt up, she had run as fast as she could. She heard Randolph yell out behind her but she wasn't about to wait.

He's probably mad about the black eye I gave him yesterday, Rune thought as she dodged between two horse-drawn wagons filled with barrels of fresh fish from the docks. *I'll give him another one today if he tries to touch me again.*

She groaned when another one of Randolph's men spotted her. She was two blocks from the orphanage. She knew the horrid man wouldn't try anything there. She was fed up with him and his demands. She had to vary her times and the spots where she sold her flowers three times in the last two weeks because of him.

Rune pushed off the wall as the man started down the alley toward her. She turned the corner and ran headfirst into a tall, lanky form. Hard hands grabbed her arms to keep her from falling. With a silent moan, she looked up into the twinkling eyes of Officer Olson Myers.

"Why, Miss August," he said in his cheerful, deep voice. "Where is the fire?"

Rune pushed her long hair back behind her ear and smiled nervously up at the officer who often came by to see the children. Sister Mary and Sister Helen like to hint that he really came by to see Rune, but Rune refused to rise to their baiting. She knew better than to encourage the young officer to believe there could ever be more than friendship between them.

"I was just on my way back to the orphanage," Rune replied, glancing behind her. She turned back with a smile and touched Officer Myers arm. "Would you be so kind as to escort me? I know the children would love to see you."

Olson grinned down at Rune, his thin mustache curving upwards. "I would be honored, Miss August. How are you doing on this fine evening? Did you sell all of your lovely flowers today?"

Rune mumbled an answer. She knew that they were being followed as they walked slowly back to the orphanage. She fought the urge to just turn and yell at the man to tell Randolph to leave her and the Sisters alone. She didn't, though. Walter Randolph might be a slimy weasel, but he was a very wealthy and powerful one.

It took almost an hour before Rune was able to peel herself away from the friendly officer once they reached the orphanage. Sister Helen had to offer him a cup of tea. Sister Mary had to give him a piece of cake. Mother Magdalene asked him how his day was and if he was courting anyone.

Rune had rolled her eyes at that obvious attempt to feel out his intentions. She had finally taken pity on the poor, blushing man and exclaimed that it was time to get the children ready for their nightly bedtime ritual. She grimaced as the Sisters all stood up and looked expectantly at her.

"Let me get your hat for you," Rune grunted out.

Rune led Olson out of the sitting room and into the small foyer. The soft giggles coming from the stairwell had her raising her eyes in warning to the line of children looking down at them. She winked at two of the youngest ones, pulling more muffled giggles from her audience.

"Yes, well, it was very nice of you to have me for tea and refreshments," Olson said, nervously rotating his hat in his hands. "I was wondering if perhaps, after church this Sunday…"

"I don't attend church, Mr. Myers," Rune said shortly.

"You don't… but you live…," Olson said, confused as he looked around at the home filled with religious artifacts.

"No, I don't and yes, I do," Rune said firmly as she opened the door. "I hope you have a very pleasant evening. Please be careful of the last step. It has a slight dip in the center and can be slippery."

Rune stood in the door as Olson gave his stammered goodbyes. She knew she had taken him by surprise with her comment, but she didn't care. She didn't answer to anyone... not anymore. She had made her decision long ago and she accepted the consequences. She didn't feel like she had to explain or answer to anyone why she felt the way she did. They would never understand anyway.

How did you explain that you had lived and died a hundred times to someone who believed that you went to heaven or hell after you died? She thought as she watched him hurry down the road.

Her eyes narrowed on a dark shadow across the street. The figure stepped out into the dim light of the lamp post. The scarred face of the man who had followed her earlier stared back at her.

Rune lifted her chin and gave the man a cold smile. She had met men like him many times before. She had fought with a man just like him the first time she had died. She had sworn as she lay dying on the cold, muddy ground centuries before that she would never bow to a tyrant.

She closed the door and leaned back against it. Her eyes went to the single pair of eyes staring down in silence at her. Eyes so much like... Rune forced her mind to close on the distant memory that haunted her still. She smiled and walked over to the stairs leading to the children's dorm. She didn't say a word as she held out her hand to the small boy who stood up as she approached. Together, they walked in silence down the long corridor.

* * *

"The local lawman left just a few minutes ago," the scarred-faced man said as he spit on the pitted dirt road next to the carriage that pulled up next to him. "I wasn't sure he was ever going to leave."

"And the young woman?" The dark figure sitting in the back of the carriage asked. "She is still inside?"

"Yes. She looked right at me," the man replied, shifting from one foot to the other in unease. "She didn't look like she was scared either."

A chilling silence met his response. "Did you get the items I asked for?" The man in the carriage finally asked.

"Yes," the man replied. "But I don't feel good about burning down a holy place. I can kill a man or that young woman if you want, but burning down some Sisters and a bunch of kids just don't sit right with me."

Walter Randolph sat forward in the carriage just enough for the man to see the cold brutality glittering in his eyes. He didn't care how the man felt. It wouldn't matter. Sam Weston was nothing more than a cutthroat he had hired down at the docks. His body would be found in the burnt remains of the building. Weston would be blamed for an arson gone wrong.

Randolph only needed the man to gather the items that were to be used and to be there. He would kill him after Weston and he used those items to set fire to the orphanage. But first... first he had a certain female that he wanted removed. Rune August had been a thorn in his side for the last two years. She had petitioned the mayor and several wealthy philanthropists to support the orphanage. His arguments that the property was too valuable to be wasted on a bunch of indigent children had fallen on deaf ears. He soon discovered that the more vocal he became, the cooler his reception among his peers had become thanks to her interference.

He had come to the conclusion that he needed to take care of the situation himself. Time after time, his meetings with the stubborn but beautiful Miss August had led to nothing but frustration, both physically and financially. She had rebuffed his attentions just as she had refused to take his money.

"You are not being paid to feel things, Mr. Weston," Randolph said coolly. "Have the items in the back alley behind the orphanage after midnight. I want to personally oversee this… task."

"Yes, Mr. Randolph," Sam muttered before he stepped back. "I'll be there."

"You'd better be, Mr. Weston," Randolph said before he tapped on the roof of the carriage. "You'd better be."

Randolph looked out the window of the carriage as it pulled away from the curb. His eyes rose to the figure silhouetted in the upper window. A cruel smile formed as he saw the figure disappear as the light inside was blown out. Tonight he would not only make the property available for his future plans, but he would have the beautiful Miss August under his control.

* * *

"Rune, where are you going?" Timmy asked.

Rune turned and pulled her dressing gown closed. Timmy had come to the orphanage a couple of months before. He was a soft-spoken boy of eight whose eyes held too much sorrow. His father had died when he was just a babe and his mother of tuberculosis two months ago.

"You should be asleep," Rune whispered sternly. "What are you doing up?"

Timmy looked down at his hands and didn't reply at first. Rune sighed and knelt down in front of him. She gently tilted his trembling chin up so he could see she wasn't mad.

"How about some warm milk and a small piece of cake?" She asked softly. "It always helps me when I have a sad dream."

Timmy looked into her eyes with a serious expression. "Do you have sad dreams too?" He asked, raising his hand to touch her cheek as she nodded. "I dreamed about my mom. She was coughing again and couldn't stop."

"It is hard when someone we love dies," Rune said sadly. "Just remember, as long as you keep them in your heart they are never really gone."

"Do you keep your family in your heart?" Timmy asked innocently.

Rune schooled her face not to show the pain she still felt at times. She often wondered if anything would ever heal the grief she kept locked away deep inside her. Being around the children and watching them grow helped.

"Yes, Timmy," Rune replied as she stood up. "I keep them locked inside my heart so I never forget them. Come on. Let's go see if Mother Magdalene saved us any of Sister Mary's pound cake. You know she loves it."

Timmy giggled and slipped his hand into Rune's. They snuck down the stairs and through the corridor. Rune decided to cut through the garden. She loved going into the garden on a clear night.

Timmy giggled again when Rune teased him about being quiet as a mouse. She was about to remark that maybe they should be stealing some bread and cheese when a movement on the other side of the garden caught her attention. There was a flash and brilliant orange flames flared up; silhouetting a form that Rune was only too familiar with along with the scarred face of the man who had been watching her earlier.

"Timmy, wake the others," Rune said, pushing the boy behind her. "Run! Tell them fire! Wake the others now!"

Timmy's eyes were huge as he briefly looked over his shoulder at the two men. One stared back at them in surprise while the other glared at them in fury. He stumbled as he turned, his hand searching desperately for the handle to the door.

"Get him!" The man with the furious expression ordered. "Don't let him alert the others."

"Run, Timmy," Rune ordered as she moved to stand in front of the door. "Save them, Timmy. It is up to you now."

***

Rune knew deep down that her time here had come to an end. She never understood how she knew, she just did. Fury built deep inside her as the pain of losing her new family swept through her. She had sworn that she would protect the children and the Sisters with every fiber of her being and she would do so.

She heard the door slam behind her as Timmy finally raced inside. She could hear his frightened voice rising as he ran back to the dorms and the rooms belonging to the Sisters and Mother Magdalene. She ignored it as the scarred-face man ran toward her.

Hoping to surprise him, she raced forward and grabbed his arm. She let her slender weight hit him head-on. He grunted and stumbled sideways when she refused to let go of his arm.

"Get the boy!" Randolph growled out harshly as he wrapped his arm around Rune's waist and ripped her away from the scarred-faced man. "Kill him."

"No!" Rune screamed.

Fury unlike anything she had ever felt swept through her. She slammed her head back into Randolph's face, breaking his nose from the sound of the crunch. She turned as his arm fell away from around her and swung her fist.

"You bitch!" Randolph snarled out as he slapped Rune across the face, knocking her down. "You've ruined everything."

Flames were crawling up the wall behind them as the wooden frame of the kitchen area caught. Rune's eyes moved from the flames back to the man standing over her. She waited until he bent to grab her again before she threw the dirt that she had gathered in her hand into his eyes.

Randolph cursed loudly and stumbled backwards. Rune's eyes narrowed in determination when she realized he was in front of the burning door. Pushing up off the ground, she charged him, wrapping her arms around his waist and pushing him through the flames. They both landed on the floor of the kitchen as it gave way. Randolph lost his balance and fell on his back with Rune on top of him.

Rune gasped as he rolled so that she was trapped under him. She barely had time to raise her hands to protect her face when he raised his hand to strike her again. He cursed in frustration and rolled off her, coughing as the smoke thickened the air.

Rune rolled away from him and crawled onto her hands and knees. She looked at him with watery eyes. Flames were beginning to roll along the ceiling of the kitchen now and the wall where the door leading to the garden was engulfed. She pulled herself up using the table. Seeing the knife that they had used earlier to cut the pound cake, she reached out and wrapped her fingers around it.

"You stupid bitch," Randolph cursed as he wrapped his fingers around the wrist holding the knife. "You could have had everything money could buy."

Rune jerked, trying to break his grip. She cried out when he squeezed hard enough to almost break the delicate bones in her wrist. He reached over and grabbed the knife in his free hand.

"Money could never buy my loyalty or make me care about a self-centered bastard like you," Rune choked out as sweat from the heat of the fire threatened to scorch her skin. "You are through," she whispered. "Not even your money can save you from this."

Rune could hear the bells of alarm and the yells of voices as people gathered to form a water bucket brigade. She could hear the sharp whistle of a policeman and the bells on the team of horses pulling the water wagon. A large beam cracked and fell behind Randolph. Rune reacted the moment his attention was distracted. She pushed as hard as she could against him. Pain exploded through her even as she watched as he lost his balance and fell back onto the burning beam. A second beam collapsed, trapping him between the two.

His screams followed Rune as she turned back toward the empty space where the door leading to the garden now stood. She walked forward, ignoring the flames. They could do nothing to her. She was already dead. She could feel the blood draining from her even as the pain from the knife that Randolph had stuck into her as he fell, threatened to overwhelm her. She wanted to reach the garden. The garden that she loved. The garden with the flowers that she grew to sell for the children. The garden where their laughter echoed.

Rune fell to her knees near the center. Mother Magdalene, who was standing in the doorway leading into the dorm area, rushed forward. She gently helped Rune down before rolling her over onto her back. Rune stared up into the night sky as the familiar peacefulness of death swept through her. The stars glittered despite the thick smoke and the red haze of the flames.

"Please," Rune whispered, looking blindly up at the stars. "Please, let me stay this time. Let me watch over and protect them. Please don't take me away again. I'm so tired of wandering. Please..." her voice broke.

"Oh, child," Mother Magdalene whispered as she brushed Rune's sweat dampened hair back from her face. "What have you done?"

Rune turned her face into the withered hand and sighed. "I promised to protect you," Rune whispered with a serene smile. "Don't cry for me, Mother Magdalene. I'll be alright. I won't... leave you... or the... children," she forced out softly before she faded away.

Tears coursed down Mother Magdalene's cheeks. She touched the still face of the young girl who appeared out of nowhere and captured the hearts of everyone she touched. She brushed the damp hair back, holding Rune tightly for a moment. She gently closed Rune's eyes with trembling fingers.

"Mother Magdalene!" Sister Mary whispered in shock as she rushed up to where Mother Magdalene was holding Rune's lifeless body. "Oh no! Oh, poor child," she cried as she bowed her head to pray.

Mother Magdalene looked up at the stars and whispered her own prayer. She prayed that Rune would finally find the peace and happiness that she deserved. Her only regret was that she had never learned what put the shadows in the young girl's beautiful brown eyes.

"Please help her find happiness," Mother Magdalene prayed. "Please give her a second chance to find someone who will love her enough to chase the shadows from her eyes."

Chapter 3

Present Day New York City

"You know it helps if you tell me when you plan to deviate from your plans before you do, don't you?" Dimitri Mihailov told the man sitting across from him in exasperation. "As head of your security, I need to know this so I can plan accordingly."

Sergei Vasiliev didn't look up from the tablet he held in his hand. His brow was creased and the scar that ran from the corner of his left eye across his cheek pulled as his lips tightened in displeasure.

Dimitri sighed and waited. He had known Sergei long enough to recognize when his friend was upset. They had grown up together on the streets of Moscow. Dimitri had been the brawn during that time while Sergei had been the brains.

A lot of things had changed since their youth. Their combination of brute force and brains had worked in their favor. Both of the men's assets were in the billions, though few realized that Dimitri was the second part of the Vasiliev-Mihailov dynasty. He kept a lower profile which allowed him to move unnoticed behind the scene. A fact that had helped in their acquisitions over the years. Neither one of them would ever forget the poverty of their youth. It was a distant shadow to them now, but the scars left behind were a powerful reminder.

Time had changed them both. Sergei was no longer a scrawny boy. The tight fit of the black cashmere sweater he wore emphasized the thick muscles under it. He had filled out as he grew older until he was almost as powerful as Dimitri. A long scar marred the left side of Sergei's face, a constant reminder that even having wealth did not guarantee safety. Guilt pulled at Dimitri. He had almost been too late to save the one man he knew trusted him.

"Knock it off, Dimitri," Sergei growled out in Russian. "I can feel your guilt radiating off you. For the last time, it was not your fault."

"I should have increased the security around you," Dimitri grunted out. "I knew there was a threat. I should have done more."

"I knew there was a threat as well," Sergei said with a deep sigh. He turned off the tablet and looked at Dimitri's face that was partially hidden in the shadows as he sat back against the limousine's rich leather. "You warned me. I was the one who chose to ignore the warning. Do not blame yourself for my own stupidity, Dimitri."

Dimitri snorted. The thought that anyone, including Sergei, could ever use the word stupid and his friend's name in the same sentence was ludicrous. Sergei was constantly referred to as one of the smartest men in the world in the major business magazines.

Dimitri gazed out the window at all the holiday decorations and the crowd of pedestrians bundled up against the chill in the air outside. He didn't say any more on the topic. It was an old argument that neither one of them won. Dimitri continued to feel guilty and Sergei became more cynical about the world.

* * *

Sergei could feel the frustration coming off his friend. In truth, Dimitri was the only human on the planet that Sergei trusted and he knew his friend felt the same. A lifetime of danger, first on the streets of an unforgiving city to the cutthroat world of the super-powerful was enough to make anyone jaded about humanity.

He set the tablet he had been working on aside and folded his arms across his broad chest. Something else was bothering his friend and it wasn't the scar on his face. Dimitri looked... apprehensive.

"I was invited at the last minute to attend a charity event to raise money. Simone and Petre invited me. I could hardly turn them down," Sergei said. "We are leaving as soon as it is over."

Dimitri's head turned and he scowled darkly at Sergei. "You could have told me," he said. "What is the charity for this time?"

Sergei shrugged. "I don't know. Probably another hospital or orphanage benefit."

"Will Ms. Ferguson be attending as well?" Dimitri asked in a voice devoid of emotion.

Sergei's lips curved, pulling on the scar on his cheek. "No. It was time for us to part ways," he responded in a hard voice. "She was making demands. It became necessary to end our acquaintance."

Dimitri's eyebrow raised in surprise. Sergei's latest lover had been the beautiful, but shallow Eloise Ferguson, a top model and a horrible actress, at least in Dimitri's opinion. She had tried to hide her greed for Sergei's wealth behind a fake smile and a camouflage of innocence. There was absolutely nothing innocent about the former beauty queen who had lost her virginity at a very young age.

Dimitri had made it his business to know everything about the beautiful actress who came from an upper middle class family. She liked beautiful things and had a tendency to live beyond her own financial means.

"What demands?" Dimitri asked.

"She claimed she was pregnant," Sergei responded.

Dimitri grimaced. Several other women had tried that same trick before. There were advantages to being a cold, cynical bastard. One was to make sure that each of their lovers were on some form of birth control and checked regularly. The second was neither of them ever let the woman they were with supply or touch the condoms that were used.

Sergei had caught one of his previous lovers purposely damaging a condom in an attempt to snare a lifetime of support from him. Dimitri had never given any of his lovers a chance in the first place. He had seen things even Sergei had not and had learned to be cautious at a very young age. Of course, none of his lovers were aware that he was as wealthy as Sergei. They all thought he was the lowly bodyguard, fit only to amuse them if they couldn't draw Sergei's attention.

"Is she?" Dimitri asked carefully. "Has she been seen by a doctor?"

"Two," Sergei replied, picking up the tablet. "The first was her choice; the second mine. I want Dr. Umberto Angelo's medical license. He took a bribe and lied about the results. It is not the only thing he has done. I will send you the information about his tax evasion and hidden accounts so you can hand it over to the authorities. Also check what he has been doing on his frequent trips to the Philippines. I think you will find he has been indulging in other unlawful activities."

"Done," Dimitri said, reaching into his jacket pocket to pull out a small notepad.

Sergei shook his head. "When are you going to come into the twenty-first century and use a computer to help you take notes?" He asked in amusement.

Dimitri scowled at the softly glowing tablet. "You know I always break the damn things," he grumbled. "They don't like me."

"Yet, you are a master at setting up security programming." Sergei looked at Dimitri again and frowned. "What is bothering you, my friend? You seem distracted tonight."

"Do you think you will ever find a woman you could trust? One that you would want to spend the rest of your life with?" Dimitri asked, glancing at Sergei before looking back out at the colorful lights decorating the streets.

"Do you mean like we used to talk about finding or just one that I can trust enough to breed an heir?" Sergei asked before a sudden ugly thought crossed his mind. "Have you… found someone?" He asked tersely.

"No," Dimitri snorted out. "I don't think there is a woman alive that I would be interested in being tied to for the rest of my life."

* * *

Sergei released the breath he was holding. They had talked about finding their perfect woman when they were younger. As they had grown older, they often compared the women they were dating with the one they wished for so long ago.

She would be strong. Dimitri insisted she would have to be to live with them, but in a good way. In their adolescent minds, she would fit perfectly between them. She would be the one to complete them and make them the family they never had.

She would also be intelligent, compassionate, loving, and Dimitri added this trait as well, a little bit stubborn. Sergei had asked why he wanted their woman to be stubborn. Dimitri had replied she would need to be stubborn if she was expected to put up with both of them at the same time. Not to be outdone, Sergei had added that if she was stubborn, than she also needed to be passionate enough to handle all the loving they would give her.

They had laughed as they wished upon the stars that night so long ago. They still talked about it on occasion, usually when they retreated to their 'lair' to regroup from the world of humanity.

Sergei looked out the window as they passed a large group of colorfully dressed women who were eyeing the limousine. His lips curled in distaste as one of the women opened her coat to reveal the minuscule dress she was wearing. He had seen the same type of women when he was poor. He had no more use for them now than he did when he was younger.

"Then I guess that answers your question," Sergei replied. "I haven't found a woman either."

Dimitri breathed out a sigh. "I have to admit I was worried you would present Ms. Ferguson as a candidate. I don't think I could have faked a hard-on with her," he admitted in distaste.

"What about Stella?" Sergei asked, referring to Dimitri's latest lover. "Are you still seeing her?"

"No," Dimitri said without any other explanation. "How long do you plan to stay at the mansion? I need to make sure the new system I installed last month is working."

"I'm not sure," Sergei frowned and thought for several long moments before he answered. "At least until after the first of the year. I have no desire to join in the festivities or attend the 'required' parties."

Sergei knew that Dimitri worried about him when they secluded themselves at their home outside of Moscow. They had bought the huge mansion together, transforming it into their primary development lab/home shortly after they became millionaires. Dimitri took over the lower floors while Sergei transformed the upper floors. Each also had homes around the world, but preferred to stay at the Moscow residence together. It reminded them of their roots and gave them time to work on some of their new software designs in privacy.

Since the kidnapping attempt, Sergei was spending more time locked away from the world. In truth, he found little to like about the world around him and preferred the isolation. He emerged on occasion to visit a new lover or attend meetings that needed his specialized attention.

Neither he nor Dimitri ever brought a woman to their home there. It was an unspoken pact that that home would be reserved for their 'wish' woman. He set the tablet down again and focused his attention on his friend.

"That should give me enough time to test out some of the new systems I have been working on," Dimitri replied. "It is not good to bury yourself there for too long," he started to add before clamping his lips together when Sergei's eyes flashed in warning. "I know… if you wanted my advice you would ask for it."

Sergei smiled darkly. "Some things are best left alone, my friend, even with you. I will be fine, Dimitri. You have enough security there to protect every leader in the world. You saw the report that we may have a possible security issue at our headquarters in Los Angeles. Someone is leaking details of the new defense programming. I want you to find out who it is and take care of it."

"Is that what has put you in a bad mood?" Dimitri asked, accepting the sudden change in topic.

"Yes," Sergei said. "You know how I feel about anyone who lies or steals from us."

"Do you want whoever it is alive or dead?" Dimitri responded cynically.

"Alive," Sergei replied with a cold grin. "I want them to wish they were dead by the time we get done with them."

"Done," Dimitri said with a dark smile of his own and jotted down a note in the notepad.

Both men turned as the limousine pulled to the curb outside of Sotheby's. Dimitri slid out of the back seat first. He looked around carefully before he nodded to Sergei.

"Make sure the jet is ready to leave," Sergei murmured to Dimitri. "This shouldn't take long."

"Of course," Dimitri replied as he and three of his men surrounded Sergei as several photographers approached from the sides.

Sergei ignored them. He knew that Dimitri had some of the best and most deadly men in the world protecting him. Nothing could get through his friend's security, nothing.

* * *

Two hours later, Sergei and Dimitri were seated on one of the Vasiliev-Mihailov's private jets heading to their secluded home outside Moscow. The auction had taken a little longer than they expected. Ms. Ferguson had shown up outside to give a dramatic performance for the Paparazzi. Dimitri had two of his men escort Sergei's former lover away while he shielded Sergei.

He glanced over at Sergei. He studied his friend with a puzzled expression. Something strange had happened at the auction. Dimitri had no desire to attend so he asked Sergei to make an anonymous donation for him while he started on the Los Angeles issue.

Dimitri knew something unusual had happened when Sergei emerged from the auction room so distracted that he hadn't even noticed his former lover trying to gain his attention. Dimitri had waited patiently for Sergei to explain what happen, but phone calls from several of his men in California had prevented him from asking when Sergei remained silent. By the time he got off the phone, they had reached the airport.

"What happened?" Dimitri demanded after the stewardess left them alone again. "Did Simone or Petre ask you to build them a new hospital or something? I've never seen you so distracted. You didn't even notice Ms. Ferguson's little performance," he added dryly.

"What?" Sergei asked, looking up at Dimitri with a frown. "No, not a hospital."

"Sergei," Dimitri said, handing his friend a drink. "You are acting stranger than usual. Either you tell me what happened or we return to New York and I find Petre and Simone."

"I bought something," Sergei replied after several long seconds. "A statue."

Dimitri frowned. "You bought a statue? What for?"

"For the atrium," Sergei replied with a frown. "It should go in the atrium."

Dimitri sighed in exasperation and took a sip of the aged brandy he was holding. He didn't understand why in the hell Sergei suddenly decided he wanted a statue for an atrium that hadn't been touched in almost a century. Hell, Dimitri wasn't even sure he remembered where it was! The mansion they had purchased was actually a former palace during Russia's more prosperous age. It contained over a hundred rooms, many still in the same shape as it was when it was built.

"Why would you buy a statue for an atrium that we never even go into?" Dimitri asked.

"I don't know," Sergei replied. "I just knew we had to have it."

"What is it a statue of and where did it come from?" Dimitri asked in exasperation. "How much did you pay for it?" He asked suspiciously.

"It is a statue of a young woman," Sergei answered before he took a deep drink of his own brandy. "And we each donated a million US dollars for it."

Dimitri choked on the sip he had just taken. "You spent two million dollars on a statue? Is it from a famous artist? Will the value increase? Who designed it?"

"Yes, no, probably not, and no one knows," Sergei answered as he sat back in the plush leather seat and looked at Dimitri. "It is absolutely beautiful, Dimitri. I will return your donation to you if you want, but I am keeping the statue."

Dimitri stared at Sergei's determined face and shook his head. Sure they both could easily have paid a hundred times that amount but having been poor once left Dimitri on the more conservative side. If it wasn't a good investment with a chance of increasing in value, he didn't invest.

Sergei sat in the plush leather seat looking out into the dark sky. His thoughts were on the impulsive purchase he had made. He frowned as he thought of the statue of the young woman. He didn't know who had been more surprised, him or Dimitri about the unexpected purchase. His plan had been to attend the auction and make a huge donation then leave. When the statue had been unveiled, he had been mesmerized by it. The expression on the face of the statue held him spellbound. The combination of innocence, defiance and steely determination made him almost believe in humanity again - almost.

He looked at Dimitri and told him what Simone had related to him while they waited for the statue to be set up on the stage. He had been unable to tear his eyes away from it. A shiver of apprehension had swept through him, as though warning him that his life was about to change.

"The statue was in the garden at St. Agnes Orphanage. The building was in terrible shape and the city was threatening to tear it down. I couldn't let that happen. It was my home for a short time after my parents were killed. I lived there for almost a year before they located my father's mother who took me in. The statue is of a young woman who lived there at one time. I don't remember exactly who she was but she is considered to be the guardian angel for all of the children who lived there. I know she helped me during the year I was there," Simone had quietly explained to him before the bidding started. "The garden is being redone into an interactive play area for the children. The architect in charge of the renovations decided the statue wouldn't fit in with the new design. The statue was donated to the auction to help raise funds for the new playground equipment."

"She is beautiful," he commented as he studied the delicate features of the bronze statue.

"From the little I remember she was a very unusual woman for her time. I just know I always felt safe when I was at the orphanage knowing she was watching over me," Simone said with a small smile.

"What happened to the woman?" Sergei asked, but Simone didn't reply as the auctioneer began speaking.

A sense of dread built in his stomach as he listened to the auctioneer give a brief history of the statue. He looked down at the program curious to see who the artist was that designed the statue. He frowned when he found no mention of the artist or any information on where it had been cast. The work was too detailed to have been done by an unknown artist.

"All I know is that she was murdered by a man who tried to burn down the orphanage," Simone whispered as the bidding began. "There isn't a lot of information on her. Just that she lived there and gave her life protecting the children who lived at St. Agnes."

* * *

"So you paid two million dollars for a statue that no one knows anything about?" Dimitri asked in disbelief. "Because you thought it was pretty?"

Sergei frowned and drained his glass. "You'll understand when you see it. I'm having it shipped immediately. It should be delivered in the next week."

"You have lost your mind," Dimitri muttered under his breath. "Two million dollars. I hope Simone is happy."

"I told you, I'll reimburse you the funds if you want," Sergei bit out. "Wait until you see it, Dimitri. You'll see what I mean when I say I could not let the statue go to anyone else. Plus, it will give you something else to do. If anyone can find out who the artist is, it is you. You always were a sucker for a mystery."

Dimitri scowled at Sergei before he finally grunted in agreement. "You better hope I turn up a very famous artist who makes this one of those one-of-a-kind finds that is considered a miracle."

Sergei's lips curved in an unusual genuine smile. "You know, I think it just might be."

"I hope your intuition is right again, my friend," Dimitri grumbled. "Two million dollars' worth of one-of-a-kind."

Chapter 4

Rune fumed silently as she looked around the tattered atrium. She didn't want to be staring at dried and withered plants that adorned the huge area that had at one time been beautiful. She wanted to watch the children as they ran circles around her while throwing snowballs. She wanted to hear their off-key singing as the excitement of the Christmas season approached.

Instead, she had been ripped away from the serenity of her former home. She had spent the last century watching over the children. The orphanage had changed dramatically over the years, but the children, despite the changing times, remained the same. She sent warmth to the new arrivals, listened to their hopes and dreams and did what she could to make them feel safe and happy.

She grimaced as an older man brushed dry leaves aside so the workmen could set her up in the center of the marble platform. She listened as the men joked in a language she didn't understand.

She would have panicked when she felt herself start to topple over if she had cared what happened to her but she was beyond caring now. She had been ripped away from the one place where she wanted to be. Until she was either pulled back to the plane where she existed in a world of nothingness or returned to her garden, she could care less what happened around her.

"Be careful!" A sharp, deep voice snapped out. "I do not want the statue damaged."

Rune turned to glare at the male who had barked out a sharp command. She recognized his voice from the room where she had been put on display. He had purchased her for a ridiculous price. She could have told him that she wasn't worth two million dollars! She had tried to send out feelings of discouragement, but if anything, he had seemed more determined than ever to own her.

Not that he ever will, she thought defiantly.

She felt half a dozen hands straightening her before they finally stepped back. She watched as the men quickly gathered the packaging that she had been stored in for the long move. She had slept through most of it, unable to bare the horrible emptiness and darkness of the crate. She wanted to rant at them to not take it too far because she wouldn't be staying long. As soon as she could find a way to convince the horrid man that she was a bad luck omen, she planned on being shipped back to where she came from.

Just you wait, she thought as another man joined the first and looked at her with an unexpectedly possessive look. *I'll make you both wish you had never purchased me. You'll be happy to send me back to my garden.*

* * *

Sergei looked at Dimitri's face with a feeling of triumph. It wasn't often that he could surprise or shock his friend, but he could tell by the stunned expression on Dimitri's face that he was speechless for once.

A low curse escaped Dimitri when the men who delivered the statue almost toppled it. He actually took a step forward, briefly reaching out in protest. The thick cords of muscles stood out on his neck as he clenched his fists.

"Now you understand, my friend," Sergei said in satisfaction. "The moment I saw her I knew she was ours."

"You are sure there was no information on the artist?" Dimitri asked as he released the breath he was holding as the men finally righted the bronze statue and started cleaning up the packing crate.

Sergei shook his head. "I emailed Simone again and asked her if she had any additional information. She said she didn't but there might be some mention of the statue in the archives that the nuns of the orphanage kept. She would ask and let me know."

Dimitri nodded. "I will see if I can find out any information as well. She is beautiful. I swear it feels like she is staring at us," he murmured.

Sergei let his eyes sweep over the figure before turning his gaze back to the statue's eyes. Dimitri was right. It did feel like she was staring at them.

Well, perhaps glaring is a better word, he thought with a frown.

He didn't remember the angry look in her eyes before. Of course, he hadn't had much of a chance to study her before she was taken away to be crated up and shipped out. Still, it felt almost like she was...

"Does it feel like she is mad at us?" Dimitri asked as he studied her face. "I swear I can feel the heat from her gaze. Almost like she is upset that we purchased her."

Sergei laughed and slapped Dimitri's shoulder. "Well, she will just have to accept that we own her now and nothing will change that. Come, let us take a closer look at our new prize."

Dimitri mumbled something under his breath, but he stepped forward toward the center platform. His gaze moved around the huge atrium. Beautiful arched windows with stained glass covered the ceiling showcasing the light fall of snow. Golden beams curved up until they reached a peak.

The workmanship was beautiful. Dozens of marble statues, many of them either Roman or Greek Gods and Goddesses surrounded the interior. A large reflection pond, green with algae, ran on the left side of the center platform which was made from the finest Italian marble. In the far corner, a spiral staircase rose up toward the ceiling where an intricately cast metal platform ran around the upper level of the atrium giving a clear view of the entire area. A gilded cage, once filled with exotic birds, stood off to the side.

"I never realized how beautiful this room was," Dimitri commented as he stepped up onto the platform where the statue stood. "Perhaps we should get a garden planner to renovate it."

Sergei glanced in amusement at Dimitri. No one would ever think the man who resembled a linebacker for an American football team would be interested in gardening. Dimitri's face held more scars than Sergei, evidence of the fights he had participated in during their youth. A small scar below his right eye, another through his left eyebrow, the crooked nose that had been broken several times and the scar that pulled at his upper lip were the ones that could be seen.

Sergei knew his friend also carried more than one knife wound and several bullet wounds, most received while protecting him from those who wished to use his knowledge. They made the mistake of under-estimating his friend's intelligence. That mistake often ended with them dying.

"I will ask Micha to have some of the staff clean the area so we can decide what we would like first," Sergei suggested as he turned his attention back to the statue. Unable to resist, he reached out and touched the bronze cheek. "I wonder what she was like," he murmured. "All Simone knew was that she was murdered saving the lives of the children at the orphanage."

Dimitri ran his fingers along the curve of the statue's neck and down to her shoulder. "It is a shame that someone so beautiful should die so young," he commented with a frown.

He would have sworn he felt warmth under his fingers. That was impossible! It was freezing inside the atrium, at least four degrees Celsius.

"I wish...," Sergei started to say as he looked into the delicate face.

"What?" Dimitri asked, watching as Sergei's expression changed from sad to intense. "That she was the one we had wished for?"

Sergei looked at Dimitri with a hard expression on his face. "Why not? Is it so hard to believe that there could be another who is selfless enough to give their life for another?" He asked with a raised eyebrow and a cynical twist to his lips.

"Yes. She lived in another time," Dimitri pointed out. "No man, much less a woman, would give their life for another unless they were paid to in this day and age. Even then, they would more than likely take the money and let you die."

"You didn't," Sergei responded quietly. "You could have left me but you didn't."

Dimitri's expression hardened when he remembered finding Sergei surrounded by the local thugs who would have sold the scrawny, frightened ten year old to the nearest whore house. Dimitri had been two years older and had been on the streets since he was eight and his mother had died of an overdose. Even before that, he had known what the streets were like. You either killed or you were killed. You either used or you were used. Dimitri had been determined to be neither used nor killed. He had been big for his age, even at eight, and had killed his first man by the time he was eleven. The man had thought to use him.

He had seen something in Sergei that had touched something in him; a knowledge that the scared, hungry boy had a chance to escape the streets. That knowledge had given Dimitri a purpose to do more than become another forgotten face among the thousands of forgotten faces. They had made a pact that day. They had become brothers, a family, and as a family, they would protect and help each other not only survive the streets but become something more.

"You are my brother," Dimitri said, turning his gaze back to the statue he was touching. "Family does not leave family."

"Then, together let us reaffirm our wish," Sergei said with a satirical grin. "It has been a year and it would seem we are both feeling a bit melancholy at the moment."

"To impossible wishes and hopeless dreams," Dimitri said as he shook his head. Still, he placed his hand over the statue's heart. "To adolescent hopes and family."

Sergei placed his hand over Dimitri's and grinned. "I wish for a stubborn, passionate woman who we can both love and who can handle both of us!"

Dimitri's husky laugh echoed in the empty atrium. "Very well, my brother. I wish for a stubborn, passionate woman who we can both love and who can handle both of us… forever!"

Sergei dropped his hand and put his arm around Dimitri's shoulder. "Now, we drink!"

"Finally," Dimitri said in relief. "You say something that makes sense!"

Chapter 5

Rune moaned softly as she rolled over onto her back. She was freezing! She sat up slowly and blinked to clear her vision. She woke to find herself lying on the icy cold marble floor in her beautiful but totally inappropriate nightgown.

"Great!" She mumbled as she rose on shaky legs. "Just great!" She growled out louder looking up at the stars glittering through the colored glass. She raised her fist and shook it. "You have a really lousy sense of humor! I don't want to be here!" She yelled out, stomping her bare foot. "Sometimes I really, really hate you."

A cry from behind her drew her attention to an elderly man who was staring at her with wide, frightened eyes. The broom in his hands shook as he stood frozen where he had been working. His mouth opened and closed, but nothing came out.

"Oh bother," Rune muttered as she raised her eyes up to the ceiling again and waved her hand at the old man. "Now see what you've done? You can't lay this at my feet this time. I didn't ask to be woken. This is all on you," she accused angrily before looking at the man who was now looking at her as if she was some sort of Goddess or something. "Definitely more of the 'or something'," she muttered before shivering again.

Her eyes swept the area before settling on a forgotten packing blanket on a bench a few feet from where she stood freezing her ass off. With a muttered oath, she glared at the man before she stepped down the cold steps and grabbed the blanket. She swung it over her shoulders and wished she had a nice pair of fur-lined boots.

You could have at least dressed me for the weather, she complained as she saw her breath in the air.

She looked at the man who was still staring at her in awed silence. Rolling her eyes, she bit back another growl of frustration. She needed to get warm or she was going to die again of hypothermia this time before she even found out what she was supposed to accomplish.

"You owe me big time for this," she muttered under her breath. "You promised I could watch over the children."

She had no idea who she was talking to. It wasn't as if she ever remembered meeting anyone or anything that had caused her to be the way she was. She just knew something was out there and it had control over her. A control that she hated and fought against every time she was jerked back to the world of the living.

She had been born before Christianity had become popular and her own people had worshipped more than one God. Personally, she hadn't believed in any of it. It had exasperated her parents, especially her mother who tried to get Rune to follow in her footsteps. Rune always had too many questions that remained unanswered for her to 'believe'.

She briefly closed her eyes and blocked the memories. They did nothing but caused her grief. She turned her attention to the man who was following her as she walked toward what looked like a covered doorway. She glanced at the old man with a raised eyebrow and gave him a crooked smile.

"I'm cold," she said through chattering teeth. "Fire?"

The man nodded his head and motioned for her to follow him. She turned in relief as he led her down another narrow path. Her eyes swept over the numerous plants in various degrees of life. She froze when her eyes lighted on a beautiful Christmas rose bush. It stood out against the other plants because of the deep green of the leaves and the beauty of the blood red roses in blossom covering it.

Rune walked over to the rose and tenderly touched one of the roses. She knew, just as she always did, that there was significance to the unusual plant. Her fingers caressed the bloom as she stared down into the perfection of its shape.

"Was this here before me?" She whispered to the old man.

"*Het,*" came the soft reply. "No," he repeated in stilted English.

Tears of frustration clouded Rune's eyes for a moment before she blinked them away and straightened her shoulders. Pulling the blanket around her tighter, she turned back to face the old man with a look of determination in her eyes.

"What is your name?" Rune asked, raising her chin to look into the warm brown eyes. "I'm called Rune."

"And I am called Micha," the old man replied with a look of amusement. "You come. I will get you hot tea."

Rune's shoulders drooped at the warm look and the sweet offer. It wasn't the old man's fault that she was here. It just wasn't in her nature to be rude to someone who was innocent of any offense but kindness.

"That would be lovely, thank you," Rune replied with a rueful smile. "I'm freezing."

"Yes, so I heard you yelling," Micha replied with a low laugh. "My office is warm. Come, леди Rune."

"Леди?" Rune asked, brushing her long hair impatiently behind her ear. "What does that mean?"

"Lady," Micha replied. "It is a sign of respect."

"Oh," Rune said. "So, where am I?"

"You are in the home of Sergei Vasiliev and Dimitri Mihailov," Micha said, opening the door to a small office.

Rune groaned as heat blasted her. She scooted in and immediately walked over to a small space heater. She lifted her right foot and held her toes out in front of it, wiggling the frozen digits. The sound of a chair being rolled behind her had her smiling her thanks as she took the offering and sat down so she could raise both feet off the cold floor. Soon, a small trash can with a stack of old newspapers became a foot rest.

"Oh," Rune moaned in pleasure as the heat began moving through her frozen limbs. "That feels so good."

Micha laughed as he walked over to a narrow counter where a hot plate sat next to a small sink. He filled a kettle and set it on top of the hot plate before turning it on. He pulled a couple of cups down from a shelf above the sink and a silver canister that contained loose-leaf tea.

Rune watched him as he patiently fixed the tea. Her eyes wandered over the tiny room. A small, battered desk was pushed up against one wall. A calendar from the nineteen forties hung on the wall showing the month of December and an ice covered lake. A shelf on the far wall contained empty pots and bags of plant food along with books on what looked like gardening.

"Here, миледи," Micha said quietly as he held a cup of steaming tea out for Rune. "Would you care for sugar or cream?"

Rune shook her head as she breathed in the hot scent of mint tea. "No, thank you. So… where exactly is this place located at?" Rune asked with a wave of her hand at the narrow window that looked out into the atrium.

Rune watched as Micha frowned as he sank slowly down into a chair that had probably been in the office as long as the calendar hanging on the wall, if Rune had to guess. She wouldn't have been surprised if Micha hadn't been there as well. She sighed and chided herself for being so…

Negative? She thought before her inner conscience spoke up. *Pissed is more like it.*

Okay, so she was pissed about being pulled from the one place that filled her with a sense of peace. Who could blame her? She would have been content to remain there until the end of days but no... some*one* had to pull her away and send her back again.

"You are in Russia. Just outside of Moscow," Micha replied slowly. "Do you know where that is?"

"Well, that explains why it is so damn cold," Rune said before she smiled ruefully at his shocked expression. "Sorry. I wasn't expecting... this," she finished awkwardly.

There was an unspoken rule, or law, that she really couldn't say anything about who she was or where she came from. She had never really understood how she knew that, she just did. There had only been one other time when she had unexpectedly appeared before someone. She grimaced when she remembered that time had not ended very well either. Being accused of being a witch was not a good thing when you were in the middle of a religious uprising.

Micha nodded as if he was used to seeing the statues in the atrium suddenly come to life in front of him. Rune's mind raced as she tried to figure out what in the hell she was supposed to do now. The last time she had appeared on the steps of the orphanage and known that they needed her help. She couldn't imagine the two irritating men who had the nerve to touch her earlier needing anything from her. They looked more than capable of taking care of any threats on their own.

"Okay," she muttered into her cup of hot tea. "So, what do I know? I know I'm in Russia of all places. I'm in a huge, freezing mausoleum that needs a forest to heat it and I know there are two huge men who are on my shit list."

Micha's choked laugh pulled her from her thoughts. Rune blushed when she saw the twinkle in his eyes. She had always had a bad habit of speaking her thoughts out loud when she was trying to figure something out. It would appear she hadn't lost that bad habit.

"Sorry," she grinned over the rim of her cup. "I was just thinking out loud."

"I will do everything I can to help you, миледи," Micha said as he folded his hands in his lap and sat forward. "What can I do for you?"

Rune shrugged her shoulders causing the packing blanket to slip down and reveal one bare shoulder. She pulled it up as the cooler air around her brushed against it. She looked at Micha for several long moments before she shook her head. It was best if he was involved as little as possible. She knew the outcome of her visit. It always ended the same... with her dying in some awful, horrible way. The less she involved those around her the better, especially the old man sitting across from her. He already knew too much as it was thanks to her 'sudden' appearance.

"I could use some shoes and perhaps a coat or jacket if you have an extra one. Oh, and a hat," she added as she touched her hair. "That helps keep the heat in."

"It will be my pleasure to bring you these items, though I fear they will not fit you very well," he replied looking at the tips of her tiny toes sticking out from under her gown where she had drawn her feet up. "I will bring extra socks to help."

Rune grinned. "Thank you," she said. "Micha, what is the date?" She asked suddenly.

"It is the second of December. It is my pleasure to help you, миледи," Micha replied as he stiffly rose from his chair. "If you will wait here where it is warm while I gather the items you need. I will return shortly."

"Micha," Rune called out quietly when he opened the door. "Please, don't tell anyone about me being here… not yet," she requested.

"Of course, миледи," Micha responded with a bow of his head. "I will not say a word to anyone."

"Thank you again," Rune said before he closed the door.

Her eyes froze on the old calendar hanging on the wall. A shiver ran through her as one date appeared to glow on it briefly before fading. She turned her gaze back to the window of the small office. She could see the beautiful Christmas rose from where she was sitting. As she watched, one of the branches shimmered and a petal fell from it. The clock has begun. She had until midnight on Christmas Eve to figure out what she was supposed to do.

She released a shuddering breath as she understood this would be the last time for her. Succeed or fail, she would not be coming back again. Her time was finally drawing to a close. A tiny part deep inside her protested. She had never felt the touch of a lover's hand. She had never known the joy of holding a child of her own in her arms. She had never known what it was to be loved.

Tears burned her eyes, but she pushed the feeling of sadness away. Why should she wish to have those things when her older sisters and little brother never had the chance? Why should she be granted mercy and given a chance to have a life when theirs was cut short so long ago? If only she had gone to her uncle's home like her mother insisted instead of arguing with her. If only she had listened to her mother and father. If only she had believed and not questioned every little thing that was told to her. So many if's...

Too many to ever go back and correct, she thought. *No, I will embrace this last time and be thankful in knowing that I did what I could to give others a chance at a life my family never had. Then, I will seek my final peace.*

Her heart clenched as another petal fell softly to the ground to lay under the rosebush. She started when the door opened and Micha came in holding an old black wool coat and a fur cap. A pair of boots, several sizes too big, were clenched in his left hand while several pairs of thick wool socks were in his right. She smiled her thanks as she let the blanket fall from her shoulders as she reached for the items. She would not have much time to solve this last challenge. It was barely more than three weeks until Christmas. She pulled on several pairs of socks before sliding her narrow feet into the boots and pulling the laces as tight as she could. She stood up and reached for the hat, tucking her hair up into it, before she picked up the thick coat. She pulled it on over her thin nightgown and smiled at Micha.

"Not a fashion statement, but it will keep me warm," she said in amusement. "Thank you, my friend. I will always remember your kindness."

"Where will you go?" Micha asked curiously as he looked down at the young woman who looked more like a child in his clothes. "It is too far for you to walk to town."

Rune shrugged her shoulders. "I don't know," she answered truthfully. "I'll have to see what happens."

"How do you..." Micha's voice died as Rune stepped close enough to press her fingers against his lips.

"I don't," she answered with a sad smile. "Whatever is going to happen will find me. It always does. Do not worry about me, Micha. I will be fine." She stood on her tiptoes and brushed a kiss across his whiskered cheek.

Micha watched as the mysterious young woman/child turned and quietly stepped out of his tiny office. He watched her until she turned the corner and exited the atrium. His eyes moved back to the Christmas rose that had not been there before her appearance. A slight, worried frown darkened his withered face as he saw a petal fall slowly to the ground. Something told him that whatever was about to happened had to do with not only the beautiful, unusual woman, but with the two men who had taken him off the streets years ago and healed his tattered soul with their acceptance of an old man's mistake.

"Good luck, *миледи*," Micha whispered. "Good luck, little lost angel."

Chapter 6

Dimitri walked through the darkened corridor, heading for the stairs that led back down to his apartments. He and Sergei had spent the last several hours drinking fine brandy. They had discussed their latest project and the issue in Los Angeles. Both of them had avoided the topic of the statue, the effect it had on them and their impulsive wish.

He could feel the warmth of the superb brandy coursing through his blood as he headed down the stairs. Even though he had consumed more than his normal limit, he was far from being drunk. Life had shown him how dangerous it was to allow liquor to cloud his mind enough that it impaired his thoughts.

He stepped lightly, not making any sound out of habit. He was familiar enough with the route that he didn't need any additional lighting. There was just enough light coming from the carefully place emergency lighting that had been installed during the renovations to this part of the palace to guide him safely down to the lower level.

He was at the curve in the staircase when a shadow passed by the foot of the stairs. He paused, his body immediately triggered into the offensive by the unfamiliar form. He couldn't make out the features, but the only ones allowed in this part of the palace were Micha, their groundskeeper, and a select number of servants, all of which should be off for the evening.

The shape was covered in a long black coat and was wearing a dark hat that hid his hair. Dimitri frowned when he heard the echo of boots against the marble floor. His eyebrows rose in contempt. Whoever it was, it was obvious they were not very good at stealth. His lip curled into a cruel smile. Whoever thought to enter the lion's den was about to discover they had made a lethal mistake.

Dimitri stepped down several steps on silent feet, pausing when the figure stopped and turned in a slow circle. The unmistakable whispered curse was in English proving the person was not one of their servants or a hired guard. Dimitri couldn't understand the words as they were muffled by the scarf hiding half of the intruder's face but the language was unmistakable.

"Dimitri," a voice behind him called out.

Dimitri turned with a curse of his own as Sergei came down the stairs behind him. "Intruder!" Dimitri growled out in Russian before he turned and rushed down the stairs.

The figure at the bottom of the stairs jerked around, staring up at them with shadowed eyes before twirling around to race back the way he had come. The loud stomp of his boots echoed as he ran clumsily down the corridor. Muffled curses followed when he stumbled on a step.

"Damn it all to hell," the muffled voice cursed. "Sorry ass sons-of-bitches. Why couldn't he have at least put some shoes on me?"

* * *

Dimitri jumped down the last few steps. He had called out a terse warning for Sergei to stay back, but he should have known he wouldn't. He knew Sergei held a seventh degree black belt in judo, but Dimitri didn't care, it was his job to protect his friend and surrogate brother.

Until the kidnapping attempt, he never thought Sergei had the inner discipline to kill someone if he had to. He knew now that Sergei was not only capable, but highly skilled in how to kill. That didn't mean he wanted his friend anywhere near danger if he could help it. In his mind, he still saw the scared boy he had found in the alley behind a rundown hotel.

Dimitri slowed and held his hand up to Sergei when the figure paused for a moment at the end of the corridor. He watched as the shadow bent over before quickly straightening. He cursed when he saw the figure turn and glare back at them before tossing something toward them.

"Cover!" Dimitri yelled, pushing Sergei behind him and covering his body with his broader frame.

"Will you get off me?" Sergei growled impatiently.

Dimitri glanced down at the object behind him. A furious oath ripped from him when he saw one of the intruder's boots behind him. He stepped back, turning to look back where the man had been. The space was empty now.

"Why would he throw his boot at us?" Sergei asked, puzzled.

"Stay here," Dimitri growled.

Sergei grabbed Dimitri's arm as he turned to head down the hallway. "No. We capture him together. I want to know who he is, who he works for, and what he wants," he bit out. "Then, we kill him."

"You are sure," Dimitri asked. "I can do this alone."

"Not anymore," Sergei said, touching the scar that ran under his eye. "This corridor leads to the laundry room. You go through the servants' entrance, I'll go through the kitchen. Oh, and try not to kill him before we get the information we want," Sergei added with a cold smile before he turned away.

"Since when did you become so tough?" Dimitri grumbled out under his breath.

Sergei's husky chuckle echoed in the darkness before fading. Dimitri waited a fraction of a second before he moved carefully down the corridor. He drew out the floor plan in his mind. He moved slowly, methodically down the narrow passage making sure the intruder had not left behind any explosive devices that might be triggered by those coming up behind him.

He stepped down the single step where the floor was lower. In the center of the corridor was the second boot. He knelt, carefully turning it over. Raising it up, he looked at it. It looked like a men's size twelve. It was old, scuffed and had dried mud on the side. He frowned and stood up.

Why would the intruder remove his boots? He could see removing them so he was quieter, but to leave them behind was suicidal! He would be trapped in the house as he would freeze to death before he got halfway to the perimeter. Another frown darkened Dimitri's face.

"How in the hell did he get into the house undetected?" Dimitri muttered. "He would have had to scale the perimeter fence which has infrared sensors and motion detection, not to mention an advance heat-signature video detection system, then make his way over a quarter mile though snow and ice past the guards and more cameras before reaching the house which is secured at every possible entrance."

Fury burned though Dimitri. He would break every bone in the bastard's body until the man told him how he had gained entry not only onto the property but into the house. If he found that someone was helping him on the inside, he would make them regret ever having been born.

Stepping up to the door leading into the huge laundry room, he pushed the door quietly open. The shadow of the man stood outlined against the narrow window that he was struggling to open. Satisfaction coursed through him when he saw Sergei's dark form step into the room on the other side. Their wayward intruder was too busy trying to pry the window open to realize he had company.

Dimitri nodded to Sergei and they both silently stepped forward. It was time to make the bastard talk. He hoped that the man would not confess to who he was working for too quickly. He was looking forward to having a little fun first.

* * *

Rune wanted to bang her head against the window in frustration, but she figured the only thing that would do is give her a bigger headache than the one that was building. She had gotten lost in the maze of corridors as she tried to find an exit. She had gone through one door only to find herself in another long hallway. After almost two hours of wandering in the dark, she was ready to start screaming.

She thought she might have actually been on the right track when she stumbled through the last doorway and saw light at the end of the corridor. She headed for the tall windows at the end of the long passage only to realize as she got closer that they were solid. She had turned to go back when the man from the auction called out to someone. She had swiveled around to find the other man from the atrium staring down at her with cold, merciless eyes. She knew what death looked like and the man staring at her had it in his eyes.

"Stupid, sorry ass window! Open, damn it," Rune muttered as she adjusted her position on the large washing machine.

"It is sealed," a deep voice commented behind her.

Rune turned so quickly she almost fell off her perch. She did fall onto her ass. Seeing both men staring coldly at her sent her backing up as far as she could until her back was pressed against the cold window. She hit it with her elbow, hoping it would magically pop open so she could just tumble out of it backwards.

Hell, snow is soft, she thought desperately as they both took a step closer. *I'd even settle for mud.*

"Get down," the leaner of the two men demanded.

Rune shook her head back and forth and gripped the back of the cold metal device she was sitting on. They would have to pry her off it first. She was not going anywhere near either of the men. She hadn't realized in her other form just how damn big they both were.

"It looks like I'll get to have some fun," the broader of the two remarked to the other man. "I was wanting to break some bones. I think I'll start with his feet. You know there are twenty-six bones in the human foot? I know how to break each one of them, one... at... a... time," he added slowly.

Rune's eyes widened and she quickly pulled her feet as close to her body as possible. She wondered if there really were twenty-six bones. Personally, she didn't want him to start counting them. She bit her lip and flashed her eyes to the other man. If she thought he might be the easier of the two, she was mistaken.

"At least he won't be able to run away again when we start breaking the other bones in his body," the leaner man said as he cracked his knuckles.

Rune swallowed and drew in a shaky breath. Okay, going out the window wasn't going to work. Her eyes darted to the door behind the men. If she could make it to the door, she could possibly find her way back to the atrium and beg for Micha's help after all. Pulling her feet up under her, she loosened her hands from the back of the metal machine and drew in one final breath.

They won't expect me to attack, she thought. *I just need to throw them off guard long enough to disappear again.*

Refusing to think what would happen if she wasn't successful, Rune tensed as both men took a step closer. It was now or never, she thought, as she launched herself off the huge metal machine. She hit the broader man in the chest.

She realized immediately that she would have had a better chance of escaping through a brick wall. What little breath she had disappeared as she hit him. Instead of knocking him backwards into the other man, he wrapped his huge arms around her and squeezed until she was sure he was going to break her in half. Scared, she did the only thing she could think of doing – she threw her head forward and hit him in the nose.

"сукин сын!" *Son of a bitch!*

Rune melted in his arms when they loosened. She didn't understand what he said, but from the viciousness in his tone, she imagined it was one of her favorite phrases when she was mad or frustrated. She dropped to her knees and started to crawl through his legs as the other man reached for her. Rolling, she brought her sock covered foot up and kicked at him. He grabbed her foot, but she was able to slip free when the oversized socks slid from her foot as he pulled on it.

Looking up, she kicked the other man in the groin as he turned. He stumbled backwards with an even louder curse into the metal machine she had been sitting on just moments before. His hands gripped the front of his crotch as he bent slightly and drew in a ragged breath.

Rune didn't wait. She rolled onto her hands and knees and tried to scramble to her feet. The long coat twisted around her making it difficult, but she was finally able to stand. She had barely taken half a step when another set of strong arms wrapped around her. She tried to head butt him as well, but he had obviously learned from his friend to beware of her head. She struggled to undo the two buttons holding on the coat. She shrugged free of it just as the man she had kicked in the balls stepped forward with a low, threatening growl.

Terrified, Rune went limp again, leaving the man holding nothing but Micha's old coat. She stumbled as she fell free before bolting for the door leading to the corridor. She thought for sure she would finally make it when she grabbed the door handle and started to pull it opened. She wasn't prepared for the two hard bodies that flew into hers or being spun around so fast her head swum. Before she knew what was happening, she found herself pinned between two hot, furious male bodies.

Chapter 7

Dimitri glared at the small figure that was curled up in the chair by the fire in his study. For the last hour, they had been drilling her to find out who she was, who had sent her and how the hell she had gotten into their home undetected. Well, they had been drilling her for the last forty-five minutes. The first five minutes he and Sergei had spent trying to comprehend that their intruder wasn't a male, but a slip of a woman who was setting off fireworks inside their bodies.

"Snow works better," she mumbled under her breath.

"What?" Dimitri bit out.

Dark brown eyes glared up at him. "I said snow works better... for your nose," she snapped back. "Why don't you go bury your head in a snow bank while you're at it to cool your temper. Did anyone ever tell you that you have anger management issues?" She had heard one of the kids at the orphanage use that phrase before and fallen in love with it.

Dimitri took a step toward her. He was ready to wrap his hands around her scrawny little neck and...

"Dimitri," Sergei said calmly. "Let me handle this."

Dimitri's eyes flashed to Sergei before he turned back to glare at Rune again. His eyes widened when she stuck her tongue out at him before turning her attention back to the fire burning in the fireplace. He clenched his fist, cursing as the damp washcloth he had been holding to his aching nose dripped down his leg.

"Who are you?" Sergei demanded, looking at the young woman. "Who sent you?"

* * *

Sergei bit back a chuckle when the woman rolled her eyes when he asked her the same questions Dimitri had been asking her. There was something about her that was just – adorable.

He shook his head in disgust. Since when did he ever think of a woman as being 'adorable'? She was an intruder. She had attacked both Dimitri and him. Well, she had thrown herself at Dimitri which still surprised him. Even now, she didn't act like someone out to do them harm. She acted more like she was... annoyed with them.

And why do I feel like I have seen her before? Sergei wondered in frustration.

"I feel like I know her, but I've never met her," Sergei said in Russian, looking at Dimitri, who was staring moodily at the slender figure curled up in the chair. "There is no way I would ever have forgotten her, I'm sure of that."

Dimitri looked at Sergei and nodded. "I feel the same way. I thought I was going crazy at first, but it is like I have seen her, touched her but..." his voice faded when the young woman turned to glare at them.

"You know it isn't polite to speak about someone in a language they don't understand," she snapped back impatiently. "If you've got something to say, say it to my face or don't say it at all."

Dimitri straightened up and strode over to the chair. He knelt in front of it so she could see the menacing look in his eyes. He smiled in satisfaction when she leaned back in the chair, a wary look darkening in her eyes as she stared back at him.

Good, I have her attention, he thought savagely.

"We could break you into tiny pieces and scatter your remains across half of Russia and no one, and I mean no one, would ever know what happened to you," he told her in a cold voice.

Rune swallowed over the lump that formed in her throat. She nervously glanced up at Sergei, who stood over her with his arms folded across his chest. Anger flared deep inside when she thought of where she was compared to where she wanted to be. None of this would have happened if they would have just left her in the garden.

Suddenly, she was overwhelmed with grief, anger and the knowledge that it really didn't matter anymore. Christmas rose, be damned. If she was going to die anyway, why extend it? Hadn't she said she was tired of being jerked around. What was the worst thing that they could do to her? Kill her?

Been there, done that, she thought furiously.

"Fine! Go ahead," she growled back leaning forward until her nose was almost touching his. "Do your worst! I bet I've already had it done before. Want to burn me at the stake? I can tell you the best way to do it. Want to stick a knife through my gut?

Piece of cake. Want to run a sword through my heart? Already done that too. You want to cut me up, go ahead," she snarled back in a low voice. "I really don't give a damn anymore."

Dimitri sat back on his heels, for once shocked speechless. The fierce determination and the way she spoke made him believe every word she said. She sounded like she knew exactly what it felt like to die. The look in her eye told him she also meant what she said. She didn't give a damn if he were to snap her neck or cut her heart out.

Unsure of what to do next, he did what felt right. He wrapped his hand around the back of her neck and pulled her forward. He knew he had made the biggest mistake of his life when his lips captured hers. Heat exploded through him, pooling low in his groin until he could think of nothing else but claiming her. She froze briefly before relaxing as he moved his lips over hers, encouraging her to open for him.

Her lips parted on a soft gasp when he touched the tip of his tongue to them. He immediately took advantage and pushed forward, capturing her in a fierce, possessive claim that surprised them both. He leaned further into the kiss, running his other hand up her bare arm to the curve of her neck. A sense of déjà vu swept over him as warmth flowed through his hand. An image of the statue in the atrium floated through his dazed mind, snapping him back to the present.

Disbelief washed through him as he slowly released her lips. He pulled back just far enough to gaze closely at her. Her eyes were closed. Her lashes lay like feathery crescents over flushed cheeks. When her eyelashes fluttered and she looked at him with wide, confused eyes, he knew he must be going crazy. There was no way it could be the woman from the statue.

The soft sound of Sergei's curse echoed through his consciousness. He glanced up at Sergei to see the haunted look of need in his eyes. Dimitri rose on unsteady legs and stepped to the side with a nod. He... needed time to understand what had just happened.

* * *

Sergei stepped forward and knelt in front of the chair. He waited until the dazed eyes of the young woman curled in the chair, a tattered black coat draped over her legs, turned from where Dimitri stood back looking at her to him. A look of confusion made her look young and vulnerable.

He gently ran his hand over her cheek. His eyes held hers, watching as her pupils dilated as the tips of his fingers traced the soft curve. She leaned her head ever so slightly into his palm, as if she needed to feel his touch as much as he needed to touch her.

"Who are you?" Sergei whispered. "I know you, but I don't. Tell me who are you?" He repeated before he leaned in to capture her lips with his.

Time seemed to stop as he teased her lips, wanting her to open for him as a bloom did to the sun. Triumph filled him when her lips parted. He took his time as he deepened the kiss. His tongue teased hers, stoking her until he felt an answering fire flare inside her as she began kissing him back.

Sergei raised his other hand until her face was cupped between them. A moan escaped him as the taste of her flooded him with the fire of desire unlike anything he had experienced before. This was not the in-control mastery that he used with his previous lovers. This was something elusive… precious. As his fingers brushed down her cheek again the feelings of having touched her, that he knew her, flashed through his consciousness again.

He broke the kiss, breathing heavily and aching with a need to drive himself deeply into her. He wanted this unknown woman with a passion that scared him to the core of his being. Never had he let his feelings overwhelm him the way they tried to now.

"Who are you?" He demanded harshly as anger over the unfamiliar feelings coursed through him. "Who do you work for?

* * *

Rune blinked several times, trying to clear her mind. She remembered feeling the terrible grief and aching loneliness overwhelm her. She flushed when she remembered what she had said. She had baited the huge man in the hopes that he would end the pain with a quick snap to her neck.

She had not expected him to kiss her. She had been kissed a few times before, but never like the way the two men had kissed her. Her body flushed and she pulled the coat up in front of her to hide how her nipples had swollen. They would be embarrassingly obvious to the men due to the thin gown she wore. A dark scowl pulled at her mouth when she thought of the fact that she had spent over a hundred years standing in a garden in her nightgown.

That was not funny, she thought in annoyance. *You could have let me keep the dressing gown over it. At least I wouldn't feel like I'm practically naked now, not to mention freezing my ass off. Oh, and shoes would have been nice as well.*

Rune glared at the man kneeling in front of her before turning her heated look on the other one who was watching her with dark, suspicious eyes. A sense of unease washed through her at the look of speculation in them. She shivered and gripped the tattered coat even tighter.

"Rune," she finally whispered before repeating it louder. "Rune August."

The man in front of her stood up and took a step back. Rune averted her eyes when she saw that the front of his pants held a noticeable bulge. She turned her gaze to the fire instead. It was safer. For a few moments, she became lost in the changing colors. Memories from her childhood washed through her as she remembered her and her two older sisters talking about the fairies that danced in the flames.

Tears burned her eyes as she remembered those simpler times. A time when she had a family. Why was she thinking of this now? Did it mean if she helped whoever needed it that she would be reunited with Aesa and Dalla?

"What kind of name is that?" Dimitri asked curiously.

"I'll have you know it is a very good name!" Rune snapped, looking up at him in annoyance. "Which one are you? The Dimitri guy or the Sergei one?"

When both men scowled darkly at her, Rune wanted to bury her head in her hands and groan. When was she going to learn to keep her mouth shut? She should have just waited until they introduced themselves. Now they would know she knew who they were.

"Who sent you?" Sergei growled out.

Rune sighed, looking back and forth between them before she shrugged her shoulders in resignation. Nothing about this trip was making any sense to her. She usually had an intuitive understanding of what she needed to accomplish. She had been fortunate that her last 'assignment', as she thought of her trips to the living, took longer than normal. She had almost hoped that maybe she might have been forgotten.

This time there was nothing but confusion and turmoil in her mind and body. She couldn't believe that either of the men in front of her couldn't handle whatever life dealt them. They were not like the children or the nuns or the countless others she had helped. These guys made her look like a toy doll in the middle of a battle field.

"I can't tell you," she replied shortly before rambling out a series of questions in an earnest, frustrated voice. "Are you guys in some kind of trouble? Having issues that you need help with? Maybe have a minor crisis or anything that you can't handle?"

Dimitri's eyes lit with amusement. "Why? Are you volunteering to fix them for us?"

Rune crossed her arms over the jacket and looked at him with a raised eyebrow. "I'm just saying, if you need help with something, maybe I can be of assistance. By the way, you never told me who you were."

Sergei muttered a curse before he walked over to the bar and poured himself a glass of brandy. He drank it down in one gulp before refilling the glass. He turned and leaned against the bar, crossing his long legs in front of him.

"You will tell us everything there is about you, beginning with who you work for and how in the hell you got into our home," Sergei bit out harshly.

"I am Dimitri Mihailov," Dimitri said, shifting so he could lean against the bookcase that butted up against the huge fireplace. "That is Sergei Vasiliev. It would help if you would explain how you came to be in our home wearing Micha's old coat and I suspect his socks and boots and a very... attractive nightgown."

"Micha?" Sergei interrupted.

"How did you know it was his?" Rune exclaimed before clamping her lips tightly together.

Rune looked at Sergei with wide eyes. She bit her lip when she realized that she had condemned the old man who had helped her. She stood up, hugging the old coat to her as she stared back and forth between the two men.

"You aren't going to do anything to him, are you? I was freezing and he was just helping me. I mean, I asked him if he had a jacket and shoes. My feet were so cold and I didn't have a jacket or any other clothes, and he was…," Rune stomped her foot and looked up at the ceiling in frustration. "You see what happens when you do things like this? You should have just left me alone! I was happy, damn it!"

"Who are you talking to?" Sergei asked, standing up and setting his glass down on the bar behind him.

Rune's eyes filled with tears of frustration. She was making a mess of things. It was all their fault. If they had just left her alone. Why did he have to buy her? Why couldn't the stupid architect design the garden with her and the playground equipment? She would have been happy in a corner of the garden. She didn't need much room.

"Why?" She whispered as silent tears coursed down her cheeks. "Why did you have to buy me? Why couldn't they have just left me in my garden? Why?"

Sergei stared in stunned disbelief while Dimitri had a triumphant look in his eyes. Rune collapsed back into the chair and curled up, burying her head in the old coat and cried for the first time in over a century. She felt lost and lonely and terribly, terribly frightened.

Chapter 8

"Is she asleep?" Sergei asked from where he was sitting.

He didn't bother turning around when he heard the door to the bedroom close. He had retreated to the outer sitting room of Dimitri's bedroom where he could pour himself a stiff drink. His mind swirled with logical explanations that would make sense of the tortured questions the young woman... Rune... had asked of him before collapsing into sobs. She had cried as if her heart was breaking. Each wretched sound shredded a piece of his defenses. She had finally fallen into an exhausted sleep, curled up in a ball on the chair in front of the fire.

Dimitri had lifted her limp form and carried her to his bed. She hadn't stirred as he laid her down on the soft covers and covered her. Sergei had watched as long as he could before he returned to the sitting room. Desire burned in his gut along with the confusion.

"Yes, she exhausted herself," Dimitri replied as he poured himself another drink. "Tomorrow I want to see the statue again."

"You mean today," Sergei grimaced as he glanced at his phone. "It is already close to four."

Dimitri ran his hand through his short brown hair. He sat on the edge of the chair across from Sergei. He stared moodily into the flames. His mind still on the soft womanly figure tucked in his bed. He wanted to join her so badly that he had actually felt sweat form on his forehead as he patted her down for any hidden electronic devices.

"How is it possible?" Dimitri murmured.

Sergei gave a short cynical laugh. "You don't really think she is the woman from the statue? Dimitri, think! That is impossible."

Dimitri glanced at Sergei before he sighed and leaned forward, resting his elbows on his knees. He didn't know what to believe. Logically, it was impossible, but... there was something different about Rune. Her questions brushed through his mind.

"I know in my mind that it is impossible," Dimitri admitted. "But where could she have come from?"

"I'll talk with Micha tomor... today," Sergei said. "He better have a good explanation as to why he would let a stranger into our home without our permission."

"Why would she ask if we needed help?" Dimitri wondered out loud. "She said she had no other clothes, not even shoes. She was dressed in a nightgown that left little to the imagination."

"It is obvious that she was sent here!" Sergei reasoned cynically. "There is no way she would have survived five minutes outside dressed the way she was. She is working for someone. Probably to steal the new security program we are working on for the Americans. Micha obviously found her and felt sorry for her. I bet if we had our security team review the tapes or search the premises they would discover her 'missing' clothing and how she got inside."

"What of her comments about you buying her?" Dimitri asked with a frown.

Sergei looked at Dimitri in triumph. "That is how she was able to sneak in," he reasoned. "One of the workers was probably bribed to bring her in the delivery truck. As far as her clothing, she planned to use her feminine wiles to get into our bed. Her 'little' girl vulnerability is just an act. She will show her true colors in the morning when she has more time to think. Just wait. I bet she will be trying to seduce us both with a flutter of those long lashes."

Dimitri touched his sore nose and looked skeptically at Sergei. "Well, my nose and balls will have to wait and see if her attempts to seduce are better than her earlier try."

Sergei shrugged. "We startled her," he replied with a wave of his hand. "Just wait. She will be different once daylight is upon us."

Dimitri shook his head as a yawn threatened to escape. "Well, I need a few hours of sleep before we discover where our mysterious visitor is from," he said, standing up.

Sergei frowned and stood as well. His eyes glanced toward the closed bedroom door. Unfamiliar doubt swept into his mind.

"I sleep on the left," Dimitri commented. "You can take the right side. That way we know she will not try to escape from us."

Sergei's eyes lit up with relief and he grinned. "It will be interesting to see how she reacts to us being in bed with her."

"I look forward to it," Dimitri said as he set his glass on the small end table between the chairs. "I want her so damn bad that I really hope she plans to seduce us both."

Sergei's eyes darkened as he set his own glass down. "You are not the only one, my friend," he muttered under his breath.

* * *

Rune rolled, again. Her sisters always complained when one of them had to sleep with her. She was a sprawler. She took up the entire bed. Arms and legs spread out in blissful abandon. Sometimes she slept on her stomach, sometimes on her back, but always taking up every inch of the narrow bed. She groaned when her foot moved again, searching to peek out from under the covers to see how cold it was. She needed to pee and hated getting up when it was cold. The trip to the water closet as the last term for the privy was called had always been a challenge on a cold morning.

She was sprawled across a smooth but hard surface. She didn't remember sharing her bed with her younger brother, Olaf. At ten and one, he was more bony than hard.

Rune's head popped up, her hair hanging down in a tangled mess around her face. She groaned when her foot encountered a hairy leg instead of a cold room. Either Aesa had become hairy for the winter or she had let one of the strays she loved so much into their bed again.

"Aesa, you better have not let another mutt in my bed," Rune grumbled. "Because if you haven't, you've got more hair on your legs than Jorundr Hasteinson."

"Who is Aesa?" A deep, all too familiar voice asked, amused. "And do you always move so much in your sleep?"

Rune's eyes popped open in surprise before they widened. She really, really needed to pee. She looked into the amused, dark blue eyes staring up at her.

"Privy," she murmured huskily.

Dimitri's lips twitched and he nodded his head to the right. "Through there," he replied.

Rune didn't wait. She got to her hands and knees and began crawling across the massive bed. She murmured an apology when she accidentally put her knee on a sensitive spot on the other warm body in the bed. Her eyes glanced up into the dark brown eyes of the man she was crawling over. He was hard as well, but his chest was covered in dark hair. She grimaced when she saw the speculative look on his face. Obviously her foot had encountered neither a stray mutt nor her sister's suddenly hair leg.

"Sorry, have to go to the privy," Rune muttered.

"Just be careful," Sergei muttered as her other knee pressed against his family jewels.

"Sorry," Rune muttered again as she half slid, half fell out of the bed. She paused for a moment before looking at the two men who were lying in the huge bed behind her. "Thank you for small blessings. Tisn't freezing!" She breathed in relief before hurrying through the door that Dimitri had pointed to.

* * *

Rune slammed the door behind her as she hurried into a room that was larger than the house she had lived in as a child. She turned impatiently in a circle before spying what she assumed was the item she needed. She breathed a sigh of relief as she emptied her full bladder. Not having a living body for over a hundred years had its advantages. She looked around the changes to the old garden robe, water closet and privy of the past. She turned in surprise when the water flushed on its own as she stood.

A giggle escaped her as she watched the water disappear. This was a huge improvement over the facilities at the orphanage. She straightened her nightgown and walked over to the large mirror where two sinks were carved out of marble. Her hand ran over the smooth surface before dipping them under the spout. Her breath caught as warm water immediately poured into her hand.

Her eyes wandered over the elegant room. She couldn't resist exploring it. A tub the size of a small boat was sunken into a platform and thick, fluffy towels hung from bars on the wall. She touched them in awe. They were so soft she felt like she could bury herself in them. Beautiful dark wood cabinets held more of the thick towels and the mirrors!

"I can see forever in them," Rune whispered as she pushed her hair back and looked at herself critically.

She saw the same pert nose covered with the hint of freckles that her father said she received from annoying the God Loki. She touched her cheek. She had her father's dark brown eyes. Her mother said they were so expressive that everyone could see all the way to her soul.

Her hair was a mixture of dark and light brown, thick and curly. She wore it to her waist as was the custom of her people. She was tall, taller than her other two sisters. Her father joked it was because she was always trying to see over everyone's head and she had stretched her body. She had the strong body of the Viking women and while she was not as gifted in the bosom as her sisters had been, it had been enough to attract the attention of a visiting chieftain. She closed her eyes and breathed away the memories before opening them again.

She turned as her eyes caught a clear room against the far wall. Curious, she walked over to it. She touched the clear door and was surprised when it slid open. She stepped in, admiring the smooth cut of the stones and how they fit together so perfectly. There was a beautiful stone seat along one wall and circular silver knobs across from it. She touched the knob and icy cold water poured down over her, scaring her so badly she let out a blood curdling scream.

She frantically fought with the clear door, sliding it open and falling out of the small enclosed room. She was trembling from the cold water that had soaked her. Her eyes were wide as she stared at the water falling.

"I've made their roof leak," she whispered in horror. "They are going to blame me. I just know it."

* * *

"What is taking her so long?" Sergei asked impatiently.

He was leaning back against the pillows he had stacked up behind him. His arms were folded across his bare chest and he was frowning at the closed door.

"Maybe she really had to go," Dimitri said dryly.

He was lying back against the pillows. He hadn't slept much at all. Every time he would start to doze off, he found either a hand, foot or an entire body on him. He had never seen anyone sleep so soundly while moving so much. His eyes drooped as he relaxed. She had been sprawled half across his chest while her feet had been on Sergei.

"I heard the toilet flush and the water in the sink turn on," Sergei insisted. "Do you think she might be trying to sneak out?"

"There is no window in the bathroom, just the clear glass looking into the enclosed garden. She cannot get out," Dimitri reassured Sergei, who looked like he was about ready to burst. "She will be out any moment."

"She...," Sergei's voice died when a terrified scream broke the otherwise silence of the room.

"дерьмо!" *Shit!* Both men growled as they sprang from the bed.

Sergei reached the door as it opened and a soaking wet Rune tumbled out of it. Dimitri pushed her into Sergei's arms even as he positioned himself between them and the door. His body was tense as he waited for whatever had frightened Rune to come out.

"What happened?" Sergei asked as he wrapped his arms around Rune's trembling body. "Was someone in there?"

"I... I...," Rune whispered, looking back at the doorway. "Your roof is leaking. I swear I didn't do it. I was just looking. I swear I didn't break it," she stammered out, shivering as the cooler air in the room brushed against her wet skin and nightgown. "It is only in the small room though. I don't think it will be hard to fix," she added earnestly.

Dimitri turned and looked puzzled at Rune. Her eyes were wide with fright and worry. Her thin nightgown was plastered to her body and even with her and Sergei's arms wrapped around her middle, her taut nipples were clearly visible through the almost transparent material.

"Dimitri?" Sergei asked, confused.

"Rune, my roof cannot leak," Dimitri replied through a suddenly thick throat.

Rune nodded her head furiously up and down. "It is! All I did was touch the silver knob and freezing water poured over my head."

"Show us," Sergei said gently as he felt her shiver violently again.

Rune nodded and reluctantly pulled away from the warmth of Sergei's body. She walked slowly into the huge room again, looking apprehensively at the water flowing in the clear glass room. She really,

really hoped they would believe her when she said she hadn't done anything.

"See," she whispered through chattering teeth. "It is raining inside."

Dimitri stood next to his shower staring blankly at the water pouring from the elaborate shower system that he loved. Sergei stood behind Rune staring in puzzlement before groaning when he saw what Rune's damp figure looked like from behind. The dark outline of her ass showed as the material clung to her. The back of the gown dipped down showing off the long line of her back and the dip of her waist. Her long hair hung down in wet ropes, making him think of what it would look like against her bare skin as he took her from behind.

"Rune, it is supposed to do that," Dimitri said, trying to hide his amusement at her worried expression. "It is a shower. I bathe there."

Rune looked at him in disbelief. "Why? It is freezing! How can you stand it?"

Dimitri slid opened the door to the shower and adjusted it until steam started to fill the enclosed area. He turned and grinned at her wide eyes. He held his hand out to her, waiting patiently as she tentatively placed her frozen fingers in his.

"See, it is warm, almost hot now," Dimitri said gently.

"Oh!" Rune breathed out as she held her hand out.

Blissfully, warm water poured over her fingers, then her palm, as she turned her hand over in wonder. She had never seen anything like it before.

"You bathe in it? How long does the warm water last?"

"For as long as the water flows," Dimitri said with a chuckle.

"Are you trying to make us believe you have never seen a shower before?" Sergei asked in disbelief.

Sergei's eyes swept over Rune's expression of awe to Dimitri briefly before he turned his attention back to Rune. Her expression was no longer one of awe, but of determination. She reached out and grabbed his and Dimitri's arm in a fierce grip.

"Out!" She said, turning and pushing them toward the door. "Out! Both of you. Now! Out, out, out!"

"What..." Dimitri said before he found both he and Sergei staring at a closed door. "... just happened?"

"She acts like she has never seen a shower before," Sergei said looking at his friend.

Both men stood staring at the closed door. They could hear the door to the shower open and close. A few seconds later, the sounds of water splashing and delighted giggles echoed through the thick door.

"I need a shower and it won't be a hot one," Sergei growled out as he turned to glare at Dimitri. "I'll be back in a few minutes. Don't...." He drew in a deep breath before continuing. "Don't let her go anywhere and don't you fucking do anything until I get back."

Dimitri nodded as another loud giggle filter through the door. "I won't," he grunted out.

Chapter 9

Sergei returned ten minutes later, his damp hair testament to his quick shower and change. Dimitri bit out that he was going to get a shower in the guest room next door. His dark glare was the only warning he gave Sergei that the same 'off-limits' was applied while he cooled off his own blood. Sergei felt for his friend as he watched him gather up a change of clothes and disappear through a connecting door into the room next door.

Sergei hadn't even bothered with dressing when he returned to his rooms, deciding his silk boxers covered enough should he run across any of the servants. He had been in almost agony the few hours that he had tried to sleep. He and Dimitri had both worn their boxers to bed thinking it would be interesting to see what Rune would do when she awoke. So far, nothing she had done made sense to him.

Dimitri returned five minutes later, toweling his short brown hair dry with a thick towel. He raised an eyebrow when he heard the singing that had started shortly after Sergei left for his shower still echoing through the air.

"She is still in there?" Dimitri asked in disbelief.

"Obviously," Sergei replied dryly. "I had a servant bring us some coffee and refreshments."

Dimitri grunted as he threw the towel over the end of the bed. "We might as well enjoy some," he grumbled. "Something tells me she might be a while longer."

"She is going to turn into a prune," Sergei remarked as he glanced one last time at the door before stepping into the outer sitting room.

Twenty minutes later, a rosy-cheeked Rune walked into the sitting room wearing one of Dimitri's thick black robes. Her nose wiggled as she drew in the delicious aroma of fresh coffee and warm pastries. Sergei closed his eyes and counted to ten, swearing he was going to need another cold shower if she didn't get that look of hungry delight off of her face.

"That was totally awesome!" Rune said, using one of the children's favorite sayings as she poured a cup of coffee. She wiggled her nose at the strong taste and added several teaspoons of sugar and a generous amount of cream to the brew before loading a plate with pastries and fruit. "I could have stayed in there all day, but I was worried when my fingers and toes started to shrivel. I hope they don't stay this way."

Both men's eyes went immediately to the tiny toes peeking out from the oversize robe. They looked at each other with a strained expression before turning to watch as she curled up in the chair she had fallen asleep in last night. It was time to get some answers.

"Where are you from?" Sergei asked as he took a sip of his coffee.

"Mm," Rune replied as she took a sip of the doctored coffee. "Here and there."

"Where is that specifically?" Sergei asked, trying not to grind his teeth in frustration.

Rune looked at him, chewing the piece of fruit she had picked up with the pastries. She swallowed and looked thoughtful for a long moment before shrugging. She picked up another piece of fruit and studied it thoughtfully.

"Let's see, I've been to Norway, England, Germany, and France." She shuddered as she said the last. "Nasty place during the time I was there. Everybody was fighting each other and cutting off heads. Spain wasn't too bad until..." her voice faded as she popped the piece of fruit into her mouth. "I couldn't speak the language so it was a relief when I left there. Then, America..." her voice faded again, but this time there was a sad look in her eyes. "I liked it there," she murmured.

"Who sent you?" Dimitri asked, sitting back. He decided he liked the look of his robe on her slender figure. "Who is your contact here?"

Rune raised her eyebrow at Dimitri. "I told you I can't tell you that and you don't have to worry about me contacting anyone," she replied moodily, setting her plate on the low table next to her.

"Why?" Sergei asked quietly.

Rune turned her head to look at Sergei with a sad smile. "Because he always knows where I am."

"How?" Dimitri demanded, looking her over. He had searched her after he laid her in his bed last night. That was why he had been hard as a stone. "You didn't have any tracking devices on you."

Sergei looked sharply at Dimitri, who shook his head in warning. Sergei knew that Dimitri has installed scramblers throughout their living areas. He wanted to make sure that there was no way anyone could pick up their private conversations. He had also had the interior of the ceiling coated to make it impossible for heat signatures to be seen from satellites.

"Tracking devices?" Rune repeated, confused. "What is that?"

"Surely you have watched some American movies or television shows that used those in their productions? Books?" Sergei added when Rune continued to look at him with a clueless expression. "The Internet?"

"What is that?" Rune asked, looking back and forth at both men.

"You've... never heard of the Internet?" Dimitri asked slowly.

"No, what does it do? Do you have it? Can you show me?" Rune asked.

Her mind raced through all the new things she must have missed over the last hundred plus years. She had watched the children and listened to their conversations, but lately they had been using devices that she couldn't really get a close look at and using words that she wasn't familiar with. There was only so much that she could see from her place in the garden and the older children had been coming out to it less and less over the past few years.

Sergei glanced at Dimitri with a cynical look of disbelief. His expression changed to impatience when Dimitri's cell phone buzzed. Dimitri frowned as the name of one of the men he had in Los Angeles popped up.

"Excuse me," he murmured, standing and walking over to the window.

Rune's mouth dropped open and she stared at Dimitri in disbelief when he began talking rapidly in Russian into a small box. She set her cup down and stood up. Walking over to where he stood, she looked at the small black and silver box he had pressed against his ear.

She touched it with a finger and leaned closer when he looked down at her with a frown. She pulled back and grinned up at him. Turning, she looked at where Sergei was still sitting watching her.

"The man who came to the garden had one of those things," she said, waving her hand at Dimitri, who was having a hard time concentrating on his conversation and trying to listen to Rune at the same time. "He was always talking into it, but I never could figure out what he was doing. I thought he was just a strange little man who talked a lot to himself. Do you have one of those?" She asked.

"Of course," Sergei replied, pulling his cell phone out of the front pocket of his pants. "Are you going to try to make me believe you have never seen a cell phone before, as well?"

Rune didn't respond. She didn't care whether he believed her or not. She wanted to see all the things she had missed out on. Each century brought new things but nothing like this. This was... magical. It was unbelievable that someone could talk into a small box and there be someone on the other end who could hear what they were saying. She had seen it where a person could tap on wires and make words with the taps but nothing like this.

"How do you get someone to talk to you?" She asked as she took the device and turned it over.

"Press the circle on the front," Sergei replied.

Rune pressed the button and a beautiful picture showed on the front along with the time. She touched it and a message came up. She looked at Sergei in confusion.

"Try what again?" She asked.

"Here," he said, reaching up and pressing his finger to the circle. "It is programmed for my touch."

"Oh," Rune murmured.

She touched one of the little pictures at the bottom. She squeaked and almost dropped the box when it made a musical sound. A picture of Dimitri came up on the screen. She looked at Dimitri in shock.

"Slide your finger along the green," Dimitri said in amusement.

Rune looked back at the phone and slid her finger carefully across the slick glass like he told her. It stopped making the musical sound and his picture disappeared. She looked back at Dimitri, who still held the small box to his ear.

"Hold it to your ear and speak into it," Sergei said in exasperation. He stood up and took her hand in his so he could press it to her ear. "Say hello."

"Hell…. Hello," Rune whispered.

"Здравствуйте, *малышка*," *Hello, little one,* Dimitri's deep voice replied. "My robe looks very sexy on you."

Rune swiveled to stare at Dimitri with wide eyes. "You talked to me! In the box, you said something in your language and you said..." Her voice faded as she flushed. "He talked to me!" She said looking back at Sergei with excitement. "Can you make someone else talk to me? Who can talk on this? How do you make it do that? Can I do that? I don't have anyone to talk to, but if I did, could I do it too?"

Dimitri's laughter echoed through the box into her ear before he disconnected the call. He slid his phone back into his front pocket. He watched as her face crumpled in disappointment when Sergei took his phone out of her hand. A knock on the door drew their attention to it. A moment later, one of the female servants led several people into the room.

"What is that?" Rune asked, feeling nervous as four other women came into the room, each carrying armfuls of bags.

"Clothes," Sergei said shortly. "We will leave you to their talents. Dimitri, I'd like to speak with you in private."

Dimitri nodded. "Cheri, she will need a complete wardrobe. Everything," he ordered before he followed Sergei out of the room. "Have one of the servants bring her to our office when you are done."

"But..." Rune's voice died as she watched the men walk out of the room, leaving her with six women who were circling her as if she was a fish and they were a shark who just realized there was a meal ready for them. "What are you going to do to me?"

"Make you beautiful," Cheri St. Fleur said with a snap of her fingers. "Starting with your hair."

Chapter 10

"What do you mean; you don't know where she came from?" Sergei asked the old man standing in front of him. "You gave her your coat, socks and a pair of your shoes."

Micha turned his sock hat in his hand. He looked back and forth between Dimitri and Sergei. His old hands trembled slightly as he looked down at them. He had known immediately when he was summoned to the office what it was going to be about.

"I was cleaning up in the atrium," Micha explained again. "One minute I was alone and the next, the young lady was there."

"And you didn't see anyone else?" Sergei asked sardonically. "No other workmen? No other containers? No bright light?"

"Why would there be a bright light?" Micha asked confused. "No, I did not see any of those things," he quickly added with Sergei's face darkened at his question. "Just the young girl lying on the center platform where the statue had been only moments before."

"Where the statue…." Sergei bit off with a curse. "Is the statue still there?"

"No," Micha whispered softly. "No, it disappeared."

"Disappeared?" Sergei asked in disbelief. "You are telling me that a full-size bronze statue that we paid over two million US dollars for has just vanished into thin air and you did not see a thing?"

"Sergei," Dimitri murmured quietly before he turned to look at Micha. "Thank you, Micha. That will be all for now."

Sergei kept his temper until the door to his office closed. "I want the surveillance tapes for that part of the palace and every entrance into it from yesterday," he snapped at Dimitri.

"I've already ordered it," Dimitri said, relaxing back against the window. "I also talked to the guards. They saw nothing out of the ordinary."

"Fire them," Sergei said with a wave of his hand. "Get ones that don't look for the ordinary. Get ones that know what in the hell is going on at all times."

"Sergei," Dimitri warned as his own temper began to build. "The security team we have is one of the best in the world. We will find out how Rune was able to gain entrance and who she is working for. It is only a matter of time. I will make some inquiries into the history of the statue and the orphanage in New York, as well."

Sergei ran his hands through his short black hair and nodded. It was not his friend's fault that he was feeling as if he was caught in a whirlpool and didn't know how to get out. He looked up at the door when a tentative knock sounded.

"Enter," he called out.

The door slowly opened and one of the servants entered and bowed briefly before stepping to one side. Sergei bit back a curse when he saw Rune standing in the door with a closed expression on her face. If he had thought she was beautiful before it was nothing compared to what she looked like now with her hair hanging like silk over one shoulder and the form-fitting black cashmere sweater dress and knee length black boots encasing her figure.

"We are in trouble, my friend," Dimitri said under his breath as he walked over to stand next to Sergei. "I don't give a damn who sent her or where she came from, I'm keeping her."

"We," Sergei murmured. "…until we tire of her."

Dimitri looked skeptically at Sergei before he took a step forward and lifted his hand to Rune. He didn't care what his friend said; he had no intentions of letting this unusual woman slip through his fingers. He would find out who she really was and who had sent her. He had to remember that he had seen things that Sergei had not… Things that could not always be explained. Sergei only believed in what he could touch and logically explain.

"You look beautiful, дорогая," Dimitri said with a smile.

* * *

Rune scowled at him and ignored his outstretched hand in favor of pulling on the back of the dress the woman with the thick French accent and even bigger attitude made her wear. She had been poked, prodded and pulled in every direction as the woman snapped out commands to the other women who quickly stole the thick black robe and left her shivering in the middle of the sitting room. She had fought having the color put on her face, but the woman had been adamant that she needed some. The only women that Rune knew that wore such things were not the type she wanted to be associated with.

"I'm not a whore," she had told the woman with a glare. "I do not color my face."

The woman had given her a heated glare right back. "You are the mistress of Sergei Vasiliev and Dimitri Mihailov. You will be dressed accordingly," she had informed Rune arrogantly. "I have never let them down and I will not do so now. Paulette, her hair. I want six inches cut off the ends."

Rune had gathered her hair in her arms, uncaring that she was standing naked as the day she was born. She would fight them tooth and nail if they tried to cut her hair off. Only a disobedient thrall wore her hair cut short.

"I am no man's mistress," Rune had snapped back, dancing around the chair. "You will not shear my hair like I am some lowly wretch. I am the daughter of a landowner and great warrior given said land by the chieftain of our clan himself. I am the warrior daughter of..." her voice faded as Cheri St. Fleur stepped forward with a determined stare. "Stay back," she had whispered.

Of course, the hated woman and her followers had not stayed back. She had been pushed into a chair and they had done what they wanted to her despite her attempts to escape. When Cheri told Paulette to cut off all of her hair if she so much as sneezed, Rune had frozen. The slender woman had a huge section already wrapped in her hand with the scissors ready.

Rune had whimpered as she heard the first slice and closed her eyes in shame.

Now, one of the reasons for her shame stood before her grinning. Sheer frustration over being thrust into a situation she did not understand overwhelmed her. She hated the feelings the two men stirred inside her. She had never felt this way before and had no one to turn to for advice. She should have had her mother and older sisters, but everyone she loved was gone. She had never felt as lonely and out of place as she did now.

"I hate you both!" Rune said in a low voice. "Do you see what those… those horrid women did to me? I look like a whore!"

She glared when Dimitri choked back a chuckle. She pulled her hair around and waved the shorter length at them. She was ready to kill them both. If she had a sword, she would have tried. Tears brightened her eyes as she stared back and forth between Sergei's astonished look and Dimitri's amused one.

"They cut my hair!" She cried out in a hurt voice. "They put paint on my face." She sniffed. "They put this, this thing on me and called me your mistress. They would not listen when I told them I wasn't. I hate you! I will never be your whore! I am the daughter of a landowner. I am…" She cut her hand across the air and turned on her heel. "I am leaving. I don't care if you need help or not. You can help yourselves."

Without another word, Rune walked by the stunned servant leaving behind two equally astonished men. She would find her way back to the atrium. She didn't care how long it took to find it. She would search every corridor until it led her to where this had all started. She hurried down the corridor, breaking into a run as she turned the corner. She didn't care what happened to her. She refused to live out the last few days of her life in shame.

* * *

Sergei cursed under his breath as he shot Dimitri a hot look of confusion. Dimitri returned Sergei's gaze, wondering what in the hell just happened. He thought she had looked beautiful.

"I swear I don't understand that woman," Sergei muttered as he watched the servant quietly disappear. "I do not know a single woman in the world who would not have been demanding more designer clothes and makeup."

"Or who would have complained about being our mistress," Dimitri commented, looking down the empty corridor.

"We had better go find her before she tries to escape," Sergei bit out. "It is below freezing outside."

Dimitri pulled his cell phone out and pressed a series of buttons. "Secure all entrances and exits. No one is to leave until further notice," he instructed before disconnecting the call.

"Where do you think she might have gone?" Sergei asked.

"Let us start in my rooms," Dimitri replied.

* * *

It had taken her almost three hours of wandering and a servant who understood enough French to point her in the correct direction before she found the atrium. After the first thirty minutes, she had begun to appreciate the beauty of the palace that Sergei and Dimitri called home. Beautiful paintings, tapestries and statues lined the many corridors. Polished marble and glossy aged wood gleamed as she wandered from one floor to the next.

Servants laughed and talked in rapid Russian as they worked in different areas. All had been polite, but none had understood her quiet plea for directions until a young man pointed her toward a narrow staircase. He told her to stay to the left until she came to the place she was seeking. Rune had given him a grateful smile.

"Thank you," Rune whispered as she took the cup of hot tea from Micha. "I hope I didn't get you into trouble."

Micha chuckled. "I have been in trouble many times in my life, little one," he said as he poured himself a cup of tea and came to sit next to her in his tiny office. "My first time was when I was but a young man. War had just broken out..."

Rune listened as Micha told one story after another. She relaxed, pulling the light wool lap blanket he had given her over her knees. She still wasn't comfortable with the shortness of her dress or the black stockings the women had made her put on. When she made a comment about what happened, Micha had calmly explained that women, both young and old, wore make-up and such clothing. It was no longer considered a mark of a lady of ill-repute.

Rune flushed as she realized that she had over-reacted. She touched her hair, which did feel better with some of the weight cut off. She had never considered that hair could actually 'feel' heavy.

"So, they were not trying to make me be a...," she blushed and looked up at Micha with searching eyes. "... a whore? They said I was Sergei and Dimitri's mistress and I must dress accordingly."

Micha patted Rune's trembling hand. "Sergei Vasiliev and Dimitri Mihailov are two very, very powerful and wealthy men. To be considered their mistress is not a bad thing. It is common today," he reassured her.

"But a mistress means a kept woman," Rune said, sitting forward. "I would refuse to be one, even if it was possible."

"And it is not?" Micha asked.

"No," Rune replied quietly, looking out of the small window at the Christmas rose. Already, she could see the bottom littered with petals and the remains of where a blossom had been. "I came here to help someone. I don't know who. I can't imagine it being those two men," she said, looking back at Micha. "They are both so... strong."

"Even the strongest need help sometimes," Micha replied thoughtfully.

"Do you know if they are in trouble?" She asked earnestly. "I don't have much time, Micha. Please, if you can, will you help me?"

Micha's eyes darkened with worry. "What will happen if you do not finish what you have come for?"

"I don't know," Rune whispered looking back at the rose. "I've never failed before that I know of but this time, I'm not so sure I'll have time. This is the first time that I've known that it is important that I not fail. It is also the first time that I'm not sure what I'm supposed to do," she added.

Micha glanced up and stood when he saw the two dark figures heading toward his office. "I will do what I can to help you," he promised as he moved slowly to open the door. "It would appear you have been found."

Rune set her empty cup down and stood up with a sigh. "Thank you, Micha," she whispered as he opened the door.

* * *

Sergei's eyes flashed with fury as Rune's slender figure appeared in the doorway of Micha's small office. They had searched Dimitri's apartment before heading to the atrium. There had been no sign of Rune or Micha the first time they had come down.

His heart had been heavy the closer they got. In the back of his mind, he thought she might have found her way back to wherever she came from. His stomach churned at the thought that Rune could somehow disappear as mysteriously as she had appeared in the first place.

He didn't say a word when he reached her. Relief choked him. Pulling her into his arms, he turned her so that she would be trapped between his body and

Dimitri. He captured her lips as she gasped, drinking from her with a ravishing thirst of relief.

He could feel Dimitri's hands sliding between their bodies to cup her breasts as he pressed her against his friend's broader form. He cupped her face, sliding his hands under her hair and twisting it between his fingers so that he could kiss her lips. Dimitri was pressing heated kisses against her neck. After several long seconds, he released her lips and glared down at her with glittering eyes filled with determination.

"You are not a whore," he said, huskily. "You are our woman. Don't you ever refer to yourself as a whore again."

"He is right, *малышка*," Dimitri whispered as he brushed his lips along her neck. "You are our woman."

"I...," Rune groaned as Dimitri turned her so she was facing him.

"You are ours," he whispered before capturing her lips with his own.

Sergei watched as the man he considered to be his brother kissed Rune. The sight turned him on until he thought he would explode. He ran his hands down along her sides until he could cup her ass.

Soon, he thought. *Soon, this will be mine.*

Dimitri reluctantly broke the kiss, breathing heavily before he pulled back. He gazed down into Rune's upturned face. He was amazed when he saw his fingers were actually trembling as he traced the curve of her cheek.

"I was afraid you had disappeared," he admitted in a husky voice. "We looked for you. Where did you go?"

Rune's lips curved upward in a rueful smile. "You have a very big home. It is easy to get lost in," she replied before looking away. "Micha explained that you weren't... he explained some things I didn't understand. I'm sorry I accused you and Sergei of trying to make me..."

Dimitri laid his fingers against her lips. "We never thought of you as such," he responded firmly. He glanced over her head at Sergei. "Isn't that right, Sergei?"

"Never, *маленький огонь*," Sergei said.

Rune glanced over her shoulder with a frown. "You two keep calling me things I don't understand," she complained. "What does, *малень... малень...* what does that word mean?" She demanded.

"*маленький огонь* means 'little fire'," Sergei replied with a smile.

"Then what does '*малышка*' mean," Rune asked, stumbling over the unusual word.

"*малышка* means 'little one'," Dimitri said.

Rune shook her head in confusion. "I'm not that little, you know. My father...," her voice faded. "I need to ask you something very important."

Chapter 11

Rune pulled away from the two men who were confusing her more and more. They kissed her and said she was theirs, but she knew that could never happen. In all the previous lives since her death the first time, she had never been tempted. Of course, the only men she ever encountered before were either not interested in her in that way or trying to kill her.

And usually very successful at it, she thought ruefully as she brushed her hand over her stomach as she thought of Randolph.

She walked toward the beautiful Christmas rose, stopping to touch the soft petals. She sighed heavily. She had never told anyone about who or what she was before. She had never had a need to but something told her she didn't have the time to waste trying to figure out what was going on.

What did it matter anyway? She thought as the petal fell off into her hand. She wrapped her fingers around it and held it to her heart. *Why does it hurt so much to think of leaving them? I have never cared before. Is it because I know that this will be the last time?* She wondered, puzzled.

"What do you want to ask us?" Dimitri said, coming to stand next to her.

Rune looked up at Dimitri before glancing at Sergei, whose expression had suddenly closed up, as if he knew he wasn't going to like what she had to say. She turned away from the rose bush and walked toward the center platform where she had originally appeared.

Sergei's muttered expletive filled the air as he saw the empty area where the statue had been set. He and Dimitri hadn't come this far when they had come to the atrium earlier. They had checked the small office and called out before turning to search the rest of the rooms.

"Where did it go?" He muttered, climbing the steps and turning in a circle in the empty area. "Where is the statue?"

Rune started to climb the steps, but found herself suddenly trapped in Dimitri's arms. His eyes flashed in warning as he scanned the empty space. His arms tightened as a shiver of apprehension coursed through him.

"Don't," he hissed quietly in her ear. "I don't want you to go up there. You must promise me that you will not."

Rune leaned her head back with a puzzled frown. "Nothing will happen if I go up there. It isn't time for me to go," she stated looking back at the platform.

"What do you mean 'It is not time for you to go'?" Dimitri demanded, turning her around in his arms and gripping her forearms tightly in his huge hands. "When do you think it will be time for you to go?"

Sergei stepped down the steps, stopping on the last one as he frowned down at her. "Where will you go?"

Rune bit her lip as she turned her gaze back and forth between the two men. She felt like a child's ball being tossed back and forth. She finally jerked backwards and stepped away so she could think clearly. Her eyes went to the empty platform, then the two men before settling on the crushed petal in her hand.

"I've never told anyone about me," she began softly, not looking at them. "It was never necessary, or wise," she added with a rueful curve to her lips. "I had already been accused of being a witch once and that was because I fought against the wrong man." She looked up at both men and grinned. "The bishop died a much more brutal death than I did that time. Lord Rathbone struck an arrow through my heart so that I would not feel the flames."

"What?" Dimitri whispered in shock.

"I had saved his beloved daughter from the bishop who had designs on not only her, but the wealth and power of her father. He considered himself above the law," Rune murmured as she looked at the petal again. "He accused me of being a witch and ordered that I be burned at the stake when I confronted him. The villagers were afraid to stand up to him. He used brute force and his small group of cutthroats to control the area. Lord Rathbone had been away and returned in time to regain control with his army. He had the support of the King. I was thankful I did not live long enough to feel the flames," she murmured distractedly.

"You think you have died before?" Sergei asked hoarsely.

"I have died many times before," Rune said, looking up into Sergei's dark brown eyes.

"You said it was not time for you to go yet," Dimitri said. "Do you know when the next time will be? You never said where you will go?"

Rune closed her fists and wrapped her arms around her stomach. She suddenly felt cold, alone. She walked over to the bench and sat down on it. She bowed her head for several minutes before she lifted it.

"I only have a short time," she replied in a low voice. "A few weeks at most. I don't know where I will go," she whispered in a strained voice. "I don't think… I don't think I will be coming back again. I think this time will be my last time."

"What do you mean, your last time?" Sergei ground out, running his hand over the back of his neck in aggravation. "None of this is making sense? You expect us to believe you have lived and died many times? How many? Where? How can you expect us to believe this nonsense?"

Rune felt a rush of anger sweep through her. She was opening her soul to him and he didn't believe her! She turned her gaze to Dimitri's face and saw the doubt mixed with reserve on his face, as if he wanted to believe her but couldn't.

"Fine," she snapped, standing up. "Forget it! I made it all up. I came here on my own for my own nefarious plans. Obviously it won't work so if you will excuse me, I think it is time I left."

Sergei's eyes narrowed on her flushed cheeks and defiant eyes. "And what were your plans?" He asked in an icy voice.

"To… to steal the statue from you," she declared waving her hand toward the platform. "Which I have done!" She said in bitter triumph.

Dimitri's mouth tightened as he glanced back at the platform before turning his gaze to Sergei's closed expression. His heart felt heavy as he realized that made more sense than what Rune had said at first. They had paid two million dollars for the statue. Had something else been hidden inside it? Something far more valuable than a statue created by an unknown artist?

"What was inside the statue?" Dimitri bit out as he turned to look at Rune with dark suspicious eyes. "Where is it?"

"Gone," Rune said, suddenly deflated. "The statue is gone."

"Where, damn it?" Sergei said, striding over to where she was standing. "What was in it and who are you working for?"

Rune winced when hard hands gripped her forearms in a bruising hold. She clenched her teeth when he shook her when she didn't respond right away. She looked up into his angry eyes in resignation.

"It is gone where you will never find it," she whispered. "Nothing was inside that would matter to either of you."

"Who sent you, Rune?" Dimitri asked quietly in an emotionless voice. "Who do you work for?"

"Loki," she whispered, remembering her father's teasing so long ago. "He calls himself Loki."

* * *

Sergei stood looking out the window of his office. He had finished reviewing the tapes for the fifth time. The video had been fine until the time between when the statue disappeared and Rune appeared on the platform. There was a section of empty video feed, as if someone had paused it before restarting it. It lasted only a few seconds, but it must have been longer. There was no way someone could have taken the statue in the few seconds shown on the time.

Dimitri had left after they had run through the video for the third time. He had received another call from his man in Los Angeles. Sergei took a sip of the brandy he had poured. He normally didn't drink during the middle of the day, but he had made an exception as disappointment and disillusionment battled for first place inside him. He had been right to be cynical of the beautiful young woman.

They had escorted her back to the room next to Dimitri's apartment downstairs and posted two guards with the instructions that she was not to be allowed out for any reason. She had not said a word after they made it plain she would not be leaving any time soon. She had walked quietly beside them.

"Just tell us who sent you and what was in the statue that was so important?" Dimitri had asked as he opened the door to the room.

Rune had looked at them both with such sad eyes that they would have forgiven her anything if she would have just responded to Dimitri's question. Instead, she had turned in silence and walked over to the window where she stood silhouetted against the dim light filtering in. They had stood at the door for a moment longer, willing her to be honest with them. When she refused to say anything, they had quietly instructed one guard to remain in the room with her while the other remained outside.

Sergei opened his left hand and looked at the crushed red petal that he had picked up off the floor outside the door. He took another sip of his brandy. His mind churned with possible explanations for the gap in the video feed they had reviewed.

He turned when the door opened and Dimitri came in. His face was grim. Sergei stepped over to his desk and touched his computer to minimize the image of Rune on it. It was of her standing in the center of the platform looking up. She was saying something, but there was no audio to go with the feed. From the furious expression on her face, she didn't look very happy about being there.

"I need to go to Los Angeles," Dimitri said with a dark frown. "The leak is bigger than we first suspected. My man has a person of interest. It is best I speak with him myself."

Sergei nodded. "We will go with you," he said, pressing the button on his desk. "Make arrangements to have a helicopter pick us up in one hour and have the jet prepared to leave for Los Angeles, California," he ordered.

"What about Rune?" Dimitri asked stiffly. "We cannot both go and leave her here."

"She will go with us?" Sergei said with a shrug.

"She will need a passport," Dimitri replied.

Sergei smiled darkly. "Since when has that ever stopped you or me? Have an emergency one drawn up here," he said with a shrug. "Perhaps there is a connection between the person stealing from us and Rune. I think an introduction between the two of them might be in order."

"Sergei," Dimitri said. "What if she was telling us the truth?"

Sergei's eyes hardened. "She was. She said the statue was gone and that she worked for someone by the name of Loki. Obviously not his real name. We will find out who he is when she and her partner discover we do not tolerate anyone who steals from us," he replied coldly.

"Let us hope for her sake, one of them talks," Dimitri said with a sigh of resignation. "I'll have one of the maids pack her a bag."

"Dimitri," Sergei said as Dimitri turned. "Make sure the nightgowns I told Cheri to bring are part of the items packed."

"Do you think this is wise?" Dimitri asked stiffly.

"Let us see how far our little thief will go to get herself out of trouble," Sergei suggested grimly.

"I hope you know what you are getting us into, my friend," Dimitri replied. "I know I will not be able to resist her if she decides to seduce us."

"Neither will I," Sergei murmured as Dimitri walked out of the office. "Neither will I."

Chapter 12

Rune looked out the small window of the jet. She had slept for most of the trip back to the United States. They had landed briefly several times, but they never departed the jet. She stretched and rose to freshen up in the elegant lavatory. A sigh escaped her as she saw the dark circles under her eyes. Even though she had slept, dreams from her previous lives refused to let her rest.

"Good, you are awake," Sergei said from the doorway. "We will be landing within the next half hour."

Rune stared at his reflection in the mirror for a moment before looking down. A low curse was the only warning she received as she was turned and pinned between his hard body and the vanity. She raised her hands to push him away, but found both of her wrists captured in his hard grip.

"Let me go," she gritted out.

"I think not, маленький огонь," Sergei said huskily. "Things could go much better for you if you cooperate with us," he said. "Tell us what we want to know, Rune. I will double whatever you are being paid."

Rune angrily jerked on the grip holding her. "I don't want or need your money," she bit out. "Now let me go."

Sergei studied her defiant expression. She was beautiful. She had washed the makeup off her face and changed into a pair of black jeans and an oversized red sweater that fell off one of her slender shoulders. He leaned forward and pressed a kiss to the smooth skin. A shuddering hiss escaped her and she tried to pull away from him again.

Sergei pulled her arms down, trapping them behind her. The move brought her up against his hard body. He pressed his hips against her.

"Do you see what you do to me, маленький огонь?" He muttered as he nipped at the curve of her neck. "I want you."

"You... you...," Rune tried to argue, but her body was doing things on the inside that she had never experienced before and she couldn't seem to think straight. "Ah!"

Sergei pressed a hard biting kiss to her neck as he rotated his hips. A sense of triumph flooded him when her hips moved against his. He released her hands and gripped her around the waist.

"Open your legs and put them around my waist," he demanded huskily right before he captured her lips.

* * *

Rune didn't think, she opened her legs as demanded and wrapped them around his waist. He pressed her against the vanity. The angle pressed his throbbing cock against the vee of her jeans. His hands roamed over her as he rocked against her. Heat built inside him as her hands moved over his shoulders and curled in his hair, pulling him closer.

"Sergei," she whimpered as she pulled back and rolled her hips faster. "I... I..."

"Come for me, *маленький огонь*," he demanded as he pumped his hips faster. "Come for me."

Her loud cry echoed in the small room as she splintered in his arms. She leaned forward to bury her face in his shoulder, but he would have nothing to do with that. He wanted to see her face as she came for him. He gritted his teeth as he continued to press up against her, prolonging her orgasm. Her legs squeezed him as she came. She melted against him as small breathless whimpers escaped her as he stilled his hips.

"She is beautiful when she comes," Dimitri said from the doorway where he had watched them. "We will be landing in fifteen minutes. The pilots have asked that we take our seats," Dimitri said tightly.

Sergei bowed his head in acknowledgment. He rested his chin on the top of Rune's head where she lay pressed against his chest. His eyes met Dimitri's in the mirror. He could see the flush of desire darkening his friend's face. He knew his own was a mirrored copy.

"Take her," Sergei said. "I will be along in a moment."

Dimitri nodded, stepping into the narrow space and lifting Rune easily into his arms. She whimpered as she released Sergei. Her dark eyes opened to stare back into his in bewilderment as Dimitri stepped out of the small lavatory.

"Sergei?" She whispered in confusion.

"Take her, I'll be there in a few minutes," Sergei said, closing the door on them.

"It will be my turn next, Rune," Dimitri warned her quietly as he turned and carried her out into the main compartment of the jet.

* * *

Rune didn't say anything as he lowered her into her seat and strapped the belt around her waist. She looked out the window at the thick clouds. She had been terrified when they had first lifted off in the helicopter from the landing pad at their home.

She hadn't known what the huge metal machine was or that it could fly. When it had started to lift off, she had freaked out. It had taken both Dimitri and Sergei to hold her down in her seat as she fumbled to remove the strap they had put around her. They had frowned when she had pleaded for them to put the odd shaped bird back down on the ground.

She had breathed a sigh of relief after the huge beast had landed. That is until they led her to another one. This one was different. It was bigger, longer, sleeker and even more plush and had only two wings on the sides instead of the top. She had tried to run, but Dimitri had his thick arm around her.

"Let me go," she begged. "Please, tisn't natural for a body to fly through the air," she choked out. "I thought we would travel by ship. Ships are good. Man was meant to take the seas to other lands. My father said that the Gods favored those who knew the waters. Surely there is a ship we can take back to America. I saw huge ones anchored in the harbor!"

"Rune!" Sergei had snapped out in irritation. "A ship would take weeks to travel to America. We can be there in a day by flying."

She had frozen and looked at him in disbelief. That pause gave Dimitri time to pick her up in his arms and climb the stairs into the belly of the beast. She had turned dark, frightened eyes up to Dimitri's dark blue one.

"And they accused me of witchcraft?" She whispered.

She turned her head and looked at Sergei when he came into the cabin and sat across from her and Dimitri. She flushed when he looked at her with a dark hunger and turned back to the window.

She didn't understand any of this. Her body tingled with awareness and a strange restlessness. Faint memories of hearing moans coming from her parent's small alcove rushed back. She flushed when she thought of what it must have meant. She had seen the animals on the farm breed, but she had never really thought of a man and a woman doing it. She had been interested in other things when she had lived so long ago. After that, she had been too busy trying to figure out what was going on and learning the changes of her new life to be concerned with it.

Rune bit her lip and turned to look at Dimitri when he reached over and threaded his fingers through her clenched ones. He continued talking to Sergei in Russian and she soon lost interest as they made their approach.

Her breathing sped up as they tilted and all she saw was water at first before land appeared under them. Dimitri's thumb stroked her trembling hand as they dipped and bounced. She didn't breathe normally again until the jet slowed and moved toward a distant hanger.

..*

"I could kill you," Dimitri said as calmly as he could. "Do you have any fucking idea how beautiful she looked coming apart in your arms? I am so hard I could take her here and now."

Sergei grimaced as he thought of why he had been delayed. He had been so hard and horny he had to relieve some of the pressure or he would have taken her right there and then in the lavatory. Instead, he had closed his eyes and imagined he was pumping into her instead of using his own hand. While he had relieved the pressure, his desire still remained.

"Trust me, it almost killed me to tell you to take her," Sergei admitted. "Tonight, Dimitri. She will become ours tonight. I don't care what we find out tomorrow."

"I won't force her," Dimitri said, stroking Rune's hand soothingly with his thumb when she trembled again. "She acts like she has never seen a helicopter or been on an airplane before."

"I assure you, there was no force applied in the lavatory," Sergei said, glancing at Rune's pale face. "And the keyword is act. She hopes to make us still believe in her ridiculous tale. Think, Dimitri! It is something out of a fictional book or movie."

"She is scared, Sergei," Dimitri insisted as another tremor shook Rune's body. "This is not an act. I know the difference between what is real and what is not."

"She is probably terrified because she knows we are on to her little game," Sergei said stubbornly.

"I hope you are mistaken," Dimitri replied in a low voice.

"It won't matter, Dimitri," Sergei said quietly. "I could not let her go now even if I wanted to," he admitted.

Chapter 13

Rune looked around the beautiful suite of rooms on the top floor of the high rise hotel. She had discovered another new thing besides the helicopter, air-o-plane and huge limousine that made her feel slightly sick. It was called an elevator.

She touched her stomach and smiled at her reflection. She had squealed when it started to rise, clutching onto Dimitri's arm in terror before she gave an embarrassed giggle and held her stomach as both men stared at her in amazement.

There are so many new things that I'm seeing, doing and learning about, she thought as she stared down over the glittering city far below.

"Where are we?" Rune asked Dimitri as he came to stand next to her.

"You don't recognize Los Angeles?" Dimitri asked in surprise.

Rune shook her head. "No," she replied faintly. "The world has changed so much. I saw some things, but I never suspected anything like this," she murmured. "The children didn't really change that much, especially the little ones. The older ones didn't come out to the garden as often in the past few years. When they did, they usually had some type of small box in their hands and were too busy looking at it to run, play or talk."

"Where was this at?" Dimitri asked softly.

A faint smile curved Rune's lips as she thought of her days and nights at the orphanage. "At St. Agnes. I came there the winter of 1889. There was a horrible outbreak of Whooping Cough that winter. The children were terribly ill. Mother Magdalene and Sister Helen had come down with it as well. Only Sister Mary and Sister Anna were still well enough to care for everyone. It was too much for them to handle alone and I knew that I was meant to be there."

"What did you do?" Sergei asked, coming to stand slightly behind her.

Rune didn't turn. Instead, she held his gaze in the reflection of the window. She thought for a moment, letting the memories wash over her.

"I stayed. I nursed them. And, I fell in love with the children and the Sisters," she replied quietly. "They became my family. Things went well for the first two years until a man named Walter Randolph decided he wanted the property that belonged to the orphanage. He tried to pressure the Archbishop to sell it to him, but the Archbishop believed in what Mother Magdalene and the others were doing. He had been an orphan himself and Mother Magdalene had cared for him. Once he devoted his life to the church, he swore he would do what he could to help her and the children that lived there."

"What happened?" Dimitri asked. "What did Randolph do?"

Rune let her body relax against the warmth of Sergei as he stepped closer, drawing her back against his body when she shivered in the air conditioning. She let the memories flow as she remembered back to a time so long ago.

"I lived at St. Agnes and worked in the nearby market selling the flowers I grew in the center garden with the children. I met a lot of people there. Some of them were very wealthy. I began petitioning for their help," she murmured before looking up at their reflection and smiling mischievously. "I was much more persuasive than Walter Randolph," she said before her smile faded. "Randolph got mad. At first, he would just come by and say unpleasant things to me or try to ruin my business. When that didn't work, he began sending some men to rough up the merchants around me and…"

"And…" Sergei encouraged when she stopped.

"They started roughing me up," she whispered with haunted eyes. "I was lucky in some ways. There was a police officer who fancied my attention. Olson Myers was a nice man who visited the children at the orphanage on a regular basis. He started coming by my stand which helped some. Randolph had me watched though," she said in a hard voice. "He came by the day before he… before I…"

Rune turned her head when Dimitri slid his hand along her jaw and cupped her cheek. She saw no judgment in his eyes. He looked at her with a touch of curiosity and something else.

"Before what, Rune?" He asked quietly, holding her gaze when she would have looked away.

"Before he set fire to the kitchen," she said in a barely audible voice. "Before I killed him. The day before I… died."

Sergei's sharp hiss echoed in the room. He looked at Dimitri, who was still staring intently into Rune's eyes. He could tell from his friend's still features that he was going to get every bit of information that he could out of her.

"How did you kill him?" Dimitri pushed in a low voice.

Rune moved restlessly but Dimitri refused to let her withdraw. There was something about the way she was speaking, the way she held herself that told them both that she was telling the truth.

"He… he and the man with the scarred face started a fire on the outer wall of the orphanage kitchen. Timmy, a young boy whose mother had recently passed away, and I were going to sneak some warm milk and fresh pound cake. Neither one of us could sleep," she choked out as memories of that night washed over her, pulling her back to that faithful night. "We caught them. I told Timmy to wake everyone. To tell them that the orphanage was on fire. Randolph told the scarred-face man to kill Timmy." She stared back at Dimitri with haunted eyes. "Randolph told that man to kill an innocent child! I rushed the man and grabbed his arm, but Randolph pulled me off and hit me." Rune absently touched her cheek, rubbing it as if she could still feel the sting from the blow.

"What happened next?" Sergei asked huskily.

"I heard Timmy yelling. Randolph reached for me and I threw dirt in his eyes. When he backed away, I stood up and charged him. I wrapped my arms around him and we tumbled through the burning door of the kitchen. By then, I could hear the alarms and people yelling. I knew the water wagon would be there soon. The knife that we had used earlier to cut the cake was on the table. I reached for it, but Randolph grabbed my arm and took it away from me." This time she absently rubbed at her wrist, as if it still hurt from where she had been grabbed. "A… a beam from the ceiling collapsed behind him, startling him. I pushed him as hard as I could into the flames. It was so hot, but all I could think about was that he wanted to kill the children," she said, tilting her head sideways as if she could still hear the sounds of the fire around her. "Another beam fell on top of him, trapping him."

"What happened? How did you get out?" Dimitri asked in a voice thick with suppressed emotion.

Rune's hand dropped to her flat stomach. A slight, sad smile curved her lips and a single tear coursed down her pale cheek. Her eyes clouded and Dimitri could swear he saw the reflection of flames burning within their brown depths.

"He stabbed me with the knife as he fell," she murmured. "I knew my time was up, but I didn't want to leave. It was the first time in centuries that I felt like I had found a home." A sweet smile curved her lips as she remembered her last moments. "I stumbled out to the garden. Mother Magdalene held me. I had never been held before as I died," she murmured in a distracted voice. "I remember looking up at the stars. They were very bright that night. I could see them through the smoke and the glow of the fire," she whispered lost in her memories. "I wouldn't leave. I promised her I would watch over and protect the children and I kept my promise." Silent tears slid slowly down her cheeks as she looked up at Dimitri. "I kept my promise until... until..."

"Until?" Sergei said, turning her slightly in his arms so he could see her face. "Until what, Rune?"

"Until they said I wasn't needed any longer," she sniffed. "Until you bought me and took me away from my garden and the children I swore I would watch over and protect." Her voice broke on the last word and she buried her face in Sergei's chest and cried for the second time in over a century.

* * *

"She is telling us the truth," Dimitri said, standing with his back to the room as he looked down over the city. He turned when Sergei didn't reply. "I mean it, Sergei," he said harshly. "She is telling us the truth."

"I know," Sergei said as he sat on the couch with his head back so that he was staring up at the ceiling. "What does it mean?"

"It means I'm here to help you," a soft voice said from the doorway leading from one of the bedrooms. "I just don't know what I'm supposed to help you with yet."

Sergei rose from the couch as Dimitri walked across the room. Dimitri pulled Rune into his arms and buried his face in her neck. A shudder ran down his body as she timidly wrapped her arms around his waist and held him back.

"You are beautiful, Rune," Dimitri said thickly as he pulled back and caressed her cheek.

"Thank you," Rune said with a shy laugh. "This... this is all new to me. I've never told anyone about me before."

"Why not?" Sergei asked as he grabbed one of her hands and led her toward the couch. "Tell us about yourself. How did this happen to you?"

Rune bit her lower lip, unsure what the rules were. She had never had any instructions. She just sort of knew what she should and shouldn't say. Now, she was at a loss of what or how much she should tell them.

She looked around the elegant room before glancing out the windows. In the distance she could see the lights of a huge flying bird as it flew over the colorful city. How could what she had to say be any more amazing than what she was looking at.

"I was born Runa Bogadottir in the year 814," she said shyly. "It has been so long since I've called myself that it sounds strange."

"Why did you change it?" Dimitri asked, brushing her hair back over her shoulder. "It is a beautiful name."

Rune's eyes grew sad as she looked back out the window. "The world is a strange and dangerous place. The third time I came back it was in 1120. I was in southern England. Not a good time to have a Viking name."

"Why did you choose August as a last name?" Sergei asked curiously.

"It was the month in which I died the first time," she replied with a shrug."

For the next several hours, Rune told them the many different things that had happened to her. She laughed when they asked her questions about what life had been like and expressed amazement that she had survived at all. They grew somber when she told them about how she had died each time, though she never mentioned how she died the first and second time. Those times, especially the first, were still too painful for her to share. She assured them that she was not in pain for long, for her death was never drawn out.

"I think it is more of a way to transition away when my assignment has been completed. I don't really know what else to call them," she explained. "I can sense when my time has ended."

"How?" Dimitri demanded.

"Where do you go? Do you ever know where you will go or for how long you will be there?" Sergei asked at the same time.

Rune broke a small piece off the roll that came with the dinner they had ordered. She rolled it between her fingers before dropping it back onto her plate. She was full from the wonderful meal they'd had of lobster, fresh steamed vegetables and rice pilaf. She thought of their questions, trying to think of how to answer them.

"I just know," she finally said with a small shrug. "I don't know where I go or when I will awake. The place I go to is similar to here but different. It is more colorful, vivid… peaceful. Time has no meaning to me. I don't see the things that happen here. It is always a bit of a shock when I come back, especially this time as so much has changed."

"Do you know how long you will be here this time?" Dimitri asked quietly.

Rune smiled sadly at him before looking up at Sergei, who had frozen at the question. She couldn't lie to them. She knew they had said she belonged to them and maybe, for just a very, very short time, she could. It would be nice to be held, to be wanted for who she really was for the time she had left.

"I think I only have a few weeks at most," she finally replied.

"A few… When will you return?" Sergei asked in a hoarse voice. "Are you sure?"

Rune looked down at her hands that she had folded in her lap and nodded. "This time is different from any of the others," she said into the silence that had fallen at her words. "I'm pretty sure after this I won't be coming back ever again," she added.

Chapter 14

Rune stood inside the door to her bedroom and bit her lip. Her hand hovered over the doorknob. She had excused herself and left after the silence stretched out into minutes. She had hurried out of the room, closing herself in her bedroom. She took a long hot shower and prepared for bed as turmoil churned in her stomach. She had needed to escape the frozen silence that had followed her last statement.

She could hear the men quietly talking in the other room as she leaned her head against the door. She bit her lip again and gathered her courage. She didn't want to be alone any more. She wanted to be held. She wanted to be loved.

For once in her many lives, she wanted to know what it was like to be a woman. What Sergei had shown her on the metal bird had awoken something inside her. She felt hot and achy. She wanted more and if it meant asking, she wasn't above that. She fingered the beautiful sheer white robe that covered the silk and lace gown underneath it.

"You can do this," she whispered to herself. "You want this. They have said they want me. They won't turn me away."

Not giving herself a chance to talk herself out of it, she gripped the doorknob, pulled it open and stepped out. She drew in a deep breath when the room suddenly fell silent. This time the silence didn't feel frozen. If anything, she swore that someone had turned on the heater to full blast.

"I want you," she said in a trembling voice, raising her head proudly as she looked at them. "I want you both."

* * *

Sergei clenched his fist against the window as he stared down at the city with unseeing eyes. He hurt. When Rune had said she only had a few weeks at most to… an explosive curse ripped from his lips and it took every ounce of self-discipline not to try to put his fist through the glass.

"We won't let it happen," Dimitri said from behind him in a voice that would have sent shivers of fear down lesser men. "We will keep her safe. She said she was killed protecting others. I will double the number of bodyguards. We will keep her safe until she feels the time has passed when she might be taken again."

Sergei turned and looked at Dimitri with tortured eyes. "I can't lose her, Dimitri," he admitted brokenly. "Why? Just the thought of what she has gone through over and over. How could any God curse someone as innocent as Rune to such an existence?"

Dimitri walked over to Sergei and placed his hand on his shoulder. They had both done their own share of cursing at God when they were younger. Their bellies had been ravaged by hunger and their bodies so cold they were surprised that they hadn't frozen to death.

"I am the wrong person to ask that question of, Sergei," Dimitri reminded him quietly. "My relationship with him has never been on the best of terms even when I did try to believe. What we have to do is make sure we do everything we can to protect her."

Sergei nodded. "One of us must stay with her at all times," he said. "I won't leave her care or protection to another."

Dimitri chuckled. "I am in full agreement. I..." he glanced over his shoulder when the door leading into the bedroom Rune had chosen opened.

Sergei drew in a deep breath. His eyes glittered with emotion as he stared at the slender figure posed in the doorway. She looked terrified but determined. It took a moment for his mind to catch up with what she was saying. When it did, the breath he had drawn exploded out of him. Fierce need and desire washed through him as her words washed over him.

"I want you," she said in a trembling voice, raising her head proudly as she looked at them. "I want you both."

"Rune," Dimitri said, thickly.

She raised her hand, but quickly hid it in the long skirt of the sheer robe when she saw how much it trembled. She licked her lips and turned her pleading eyes on Sergei. Taking a tentative step forward, she determinedly held her hands out in front of her.

"Please," she whispered. "I don't want to be alone anymore. What you did with me on the metal bird... I've never felt anything like that before. You said you wanted me. You both said I was yours," she said, looking at Dimitri with a pleading look. "Please don't turn me away. I know what I told you sounds crazy, but it is true. I swear on my heart that every word was the truth," she added, placing one delicate hand over her heart. "I want to feel alive… for just a little while."

Sergei strode across the living room. He cupped her face, staring down for a fraction of a second before he kissed her with a burning hunger. Rune's hands moved up over his shoulders, gripping him tightly as she rose on her tiptoes to meet him half way. The feel of a second pair of hands on her hips drew a soft moan from her. When she felt a second pair of lips on her neck, she arched backwards into the hard body.

"Tonight," Dimitri began in a voice husky with need.

"Forever," Sergei said, breaking the kiss to look at Dimitri before he looked down into Rune's dazed eyes. "This is for more than tonight or a few weeks, Rune. This is forever."

Rune melted back against Dimitri as his arms swept her up against his broad chest. She looked over Dimitri's shoulder as he turned to carry her back into her bedroom. Her heart ached that she could not give them more than a few weeks. She might not be able to promise them forever, but she would give them everything she had as long as she could.

"I promise to stay as long as I can," she whispered.

Sergei's eyes flashed at her evasive response to his demand. He followed Dimitri into the bedroom and stood to the side as Dimitri gently set her down on her feet. His fingers went to the buttons of his shirt.

He held her eyes as he undid each one. His eyes darkened to a deeper blue in answer to the heat in her eyes as she followed the path of the undone buttons.

"You are sure of this, *маленький огонь*?" He asked thickly as Dimitri's hands went to the belt of her robe.

"Yes," she whispered. "I have never been more sure of anything in my life."

She looked at Dimitri's strained expression. Unable to resist, she reached out and tenderly touched his cheek. She would never get tired of touching him or Sergei. They were both different and yet the same. Her fingers traced a small scar that ran near his temple before moving down to the one near his left eye.

Dimitri's hands froze on the belt to her robe as she gently touched him. "Rune," he warned thickly. "I do not have much control right now."

She gazed up at Dimitri. "So much life is told in your face," she murmured tracing the faint scar under his eye.

"My life has not always been one of wealth," he replied, pressing a kiss to the inside of her wrist. "I have had to kill before, Rune. You should know what type of man I am."

Rune smiled tenderly. "You are a warrior and a warrior will kill to defend those who cannot defend themselves. I have killed before as well. I am my father's daughter and I am not ashamed of it. You are a warrior, Dimitri. There is a difference between that and one who kills because they can," she assured him.

"You are not frightened?" Sergei asked, stepping closer.

"I am not from your time, Sergei," she reminded him. "I have lived during times when it was kill or be killed. I would never judge one who did what was necessary to survive."

"I am falling in love with you, Rune," Dimitri groaned out hoarsely before pulling her into his arms and capturing her lips with his.

Sergei watched as Dimitri ravaged Rune's lips. He watched as Dimitri's large hands ran down her body to cup her ass, pulling her up against him. He was surprised at the emotion he felt rushing through him. He would have thought he would be jealous. Instead, he felt intense satisfaction. This was right. This is what they had always dreamed of finding. A woman who would complete them.

He shrugged his shirt off before stepping up beside them. He reached out his hand and threaded his fingers through Rune's long, curly hair. With a slight tug, he let her know that he wanted her attention. The moment she broke the kiss, he turned her face to his and captured her lips.

"Sergei," Dimitri muttered roughly under his breath. "She is made for us."

Sergei reluctantly released his grip on her. "You bet your ass she is," he replied hoarsely as she fell against him when Dimitri stepped back to remove his clothes.

"Take her gown off of her," Dimitri demanded as he pushed his pants down and kicked them aside.

"You better not be wanting to take her slowly this first time because I have to tell you, I don't think I will last long."

"We will take it as slow as Rune wishes," Sergei said, brushing his knuckles along her cheek. "You will tell us if we do anything that frightens you or if you need more time, yes?"

A rosy blush covered Rune's face as she glanced at Dimitri, who stood proudly in the nude. Her eyes roamed his broad form. He wasn't handsome in a classical way. There was an air of danger, of untamed violence, that surrounded him.

He wasn't as tall as Sergei and his body was thickly muscled. He had numerous scars across his smooth chest from the battles he had faced during his lifetime. Rune knew enough of battle scars to know that several had been grievous wounds. She ached to explore each and every one of them.

Her eyes hungrily roamed his figure. A small smile of feminine satisfaction lit her eyes when she saw how his manhood stood out, evidence of his desire for her. She looked up at him, pleasure darkening her eyes to a richer shade of brown as she returned his challenging stare.

"Rune wishes for her men to take her as a warrior would take his mate," she said, straightening her shoulders and tossing her hair proudly behind her. "I am the daughter of a Viking warrior. I would expect nothing less."

"You have until the count of three to get undressed, Sergei, or you are going to be watching me take *our* mate," Dimitri growled out as he reached over and ripped the silky gown down the front.

Chapter 15

Rune gasped as the tattered remains of her gown floated to the floor and she found herself pressed up against hot male flesh. Fire exploded inside her as she wrapped her arms around Dimitri's neck as he lifted her. She pressed her lips against his neck, touching the tip of her tongue to his hot skin.

Dimitri's choked curse filled the air as they tumbled down onto the bed. His large hands ran over her body, causing her to press upward into him. She loved the way his calloused palms felt against her skin.

"More, Dimitri," she demanded. "I want you to touch me all over. I love the way your hands feel against my skin."

"How do you like the feel of mine?" Sergei asked as he sank down next to her and Dimitri.

"Why don't you show me and I'll tell you," she said with a slow smile as she reached out to run her fingers through the hair covering his chest. "Kiss me."

Sergei's eyes widened at her hot demand. He was not used to a woman telling him what to do in the bedroom. Every time he thought he was beginning to understand this unusual female, she would do something totally out of the ordinary.

He bent to capture her lips at the same time as Dimitri captured her left breast between his lips. He kissed her deeply when she opened her mouth to gasp. His hand moved to her right breast and he tweaked the taut tip.

"Keep that up, Sergei," Dimitri said, moving further down her body. "She likes that."

Sergei broke his kiss and glared down at Dimitri. "I can take orders from her, but do not tell me what to do in the bedroom, my friend. I think I can more than keep up with you."

"Why don't you show me what you both can do?" Rune asked breathlessly as Dimitri parted her legs and slid his palms up under her ass "What are you...."

Dimitri's soft laugh blew warm air over her clit before that warmth turned into an inferno as his lips and tongue went to work on her. Her cry echoed as she bucked at the unexpected pleasure sweeping through her.

"She likes that as well, Dimitri," Sergei growled watching as his friend and surrogate brother lapped at Rune's hot core. "I want to see her bare," he said huskily.

Dimitri broke off just long enough to replace his tongue with his fingers. "Later," he replied, glaring up at Sergei. "There is no way I could wait this time."

"What is bare?" Rune gasped as she bowed upward as Dimitri slid two of his thick fingers into her narrow vaginal channel. "Oh!"

"Open your mouth," Sergei demanded as he pinched both of her nipples at the same time as Dimitri pushed deeper.

Rune opened her mouth, not understanding exactly what was expected of her. When Sergei pressed the tip of his swollen cock against her lips, she touched the bulbous end of it with her tongue as she looked up at him for guidance. He squeezed both nipples and nodded down at her.

"Take me in your mouth," he murmured. "Have you ever done this before?"

Rune shook her slightly back and forth. The movement brushed his swollen cock along her lips, coating them with a slight film of his pre-cum. A moan escaped both of them at the same time as a curse exploded from Dimitri.

"Sergei," Dimitri said hoarsely. "She is a fucking virgin."

Sergei's eyes turned to lock with Dimitri's in stunned disbelief. "You are sure?" He asked harshly before turning his attention to Rune who was caressing his cock with her tongue. "You are a virgin?" He asked her.

"Mm, yes," she replied as she licked the tip of his cock again. "I had not hand-fasted with anyone before… you know," she replied. "None ever made me feel like this or I would have," she groaned, moving restlessly as Dimitri's fingers froze deep inside her. "I want to feel what you did to me on the metal bird again. Can it happen more than once?"

"Can it happen…" Dimitri's eyes gleamed with enjoyment and passion as he grinned up at Sergei. "I think we need to show her just how many times she can feel that way again."

"Do it," Sergei gritted out, turning his attention back to Rune who had taken the entire tip of his cock in her mouth and was sucking on it. "But damn it, you'd better hurry."

"With pleasure," Dimitri muttered.

* * *

Rune never knew such pleasure existed in the universe. Her body was burning and so sensitive even the sheets under her were driving her crazy. Dimitri had her legs spread open for him and the feel of his teeth and tongue caressing her in her woman's area made her wonder what other things she had missed.

He pressed his fingers deep into her again. She felt a brief discomfort before it was gone. The pain changed to something much worse – a pleasure that had her trembling as he continued to lap at the nub hidden in her slick folds while he pushed his fingers deep into her.

She slipped her hand up to grasp Sergei's long shaft at the same time as she turned her face into his leg and screamed out as pleasure exploded through her. Her body rose up as she felt Dimitri shift so that he was kneeling between her trembling legs now. His massive hands wrapped under her thighs as he aligned his throbbing shaft with her pulsing vaginal channel.

"Now, I take you," Dimitri said pushing forward. "Yes!" He hissed out.

Sergei watched as Dimitri claimed Rune for the first time. His cock bobbed up and down as he watched the beautiful sight. His attention moved to Rune when he felt her hand tighten around his cock, gripping it like he imagined her pussy would.

"Take me," he whispered, looking down into her eyes.

Rune stroked him, using the same rhythm that Dimitri was using with her. Long strokes, then short, quick ones followed by longer ones. Each one she moved her lips over the tip and slid his cock further down her throat.

"Так красиво. Ты наш красивая статуя, наш ангел, наш женщина." *So beautiful. You are our beautiful statue, our angel, our woman,* Dimitri muttered as he watched her.

"Yes, so beautiful," Sergei agreed hoarsely.

Rune reached her other hand over to caress Sergei's heavy sack, massaging it gently and exploring it as it grew tighter and tighter. His loud cry and the almost painful pinch of his fingers on her nipples were the only warning she had before he exploded in her mouth. Unsure of what to do, she drank him down.

"Rune!" Dimitri's loud cry followed as he pumped deeply into her before exploding as well.

Rune closed her eyes and squeezed Sergei tightly as her body came apart again around Dimitri. The feel of him pulsing deep into her already over-sensitive vagina left her melting around him.

She slowly released Sergei. She looked up at him when he shuddered as he slid from her mouth. His dark brown eyes opened and he stared down at her with such a look of possessive passion, that for a moment, Rune could almost believe that he loved her.

Her eyes moved to Dimitri. He stared back at her. His dark blue eyes were heated as well, leaving her in no doubt that she was his.

"That was incredible," she whispered.

Dimitri chuckled and looked up at Sergei. "That is just the beginning, мало четыре," he said. "We are just beginning."

Rune sighed heavily as Dimitri slowly pulled out of her. "I am really going to have to learn Russian so I can understand all the names you two call me," she complained.

Sergei threaded his fingers through her hair and turned her head to look up at him. He searched her face carefully before he bent over and gave her a brief kiss. He liked the taste of him on her lips. It re-enforced that she belonged to him and Dimitri.

"The only name you need to understand is that you are ours, Rune," Sergei said roughly. "Never forget that. We have claimed you and we do not give up what belongs to us."

Chapter 16

"Hold her," groaned Dimitri as Rune rolled again. "I don't think I have ever seen anyone move so much in their sleep."

Sergei chuckled as he wrapped his arm around Rune's waist and pulled her back against him. Her leg immediately wound around the one he slid between her long limbs and she sighed as her arm flew over to Dimitri's vacant pillow.

"Dimitri!" She cried out, jerking partially awake.

She struggled to sit up as a drowsy panic flooded her. She pushed her hair out of her eyes and looked wildly around for him. She started to crawl from the bed, but strong arms wrapped around her.

"Hush, малышка," Sergei soothed, pulling her back into his arms. "He will be back. His cell phone was ringing."

"Cell phone?" Rune mumbled, looking around the room in confusion.

"The little box that you can speak into and others can speak to you," Sergei reminded her in amusement.

"Oh, cell phone," she muttered, falling back down and snuggling up next to Sergei's warm body. "Want one but don't have anyone to talk to," she mumbled already half asleep again.

"You have Dimitri and me," Sergei whispered gently in her ear.

"I like that," she murmured, yawning widely before snuggling her ass deeper into Sergei. "Sleep."

Sergei gritted his teeth as he felt her rounded ass pushing into his erection. His arousal had nothing to do with an early morning erection and everything to do with the lush naked woman in his arms. His hand slid up her belly to her breasts. His fingers wrapped around the taut nipple of her right breast.

"I want to wake you up," he murmured, running his lips along her shoulder as he pressed his arousal against her. "You have definitely woken me up."

"Sergei," she moaned and moved restlessly.

Sergei rolled, forcing Rune over onto her stomach as he came up on top of her. Kneeling in between her spread legs, he gripped her hips and pulled her up onto her knees. A loud groan was the only warning she got before he aligned himself with her and pushed forward until he was buried as deeply as he could go. He kept one arm wrapped around her waist so she wouldn't collapse. He held onto the headboard with his other hand as he caged her body with his own.

"Sergei!" Rune's muffled cry echoed as he began rocking back and forth.

"Yes, Rune," Sergei groaned loudly. "You feel so good."

Sergei gritted his teeth as he rode her slowly in the hopes that he could hold out long enough for Dimitri to get off the damn phone and join them. The feel of his cock sliding back and forth against her hot channel caused beads of sweat to form on his brow as he fought to prolong his orgasm.

"Damn you, Dimitri," Sergei muttered darkly. "Hurry!"

"With pleasure," Dimitri's gruff voice replied as he tossed his cell phone onto the chair. "She looks so damn beautiful being fucked from behind."

"Let's see how she looks being fucked from behind while she is sucking your cock," Sergei said. "I bet she is even more beautiful."

Dimitri didn't need a second encouragement. He slid onto the bed near the headboard. Sergei wrapped his hands around Rune until he was cupping both of her breasts. He leaned back on his heels, pulling her back with him.

"Oh ancient Gods," Rune moaned as Sergei's long, thick cock went so deep she swore she could feel it pressing against her womb. "Sergei!"

Sergei squeezed his hands at the same time as he rocked his hips. He waited until Dimitri was in position before he released her breasts. He slid his right hand down to her waist as he wrapped her hair in his left hand. He wanted to watch her slide Dimitri's thick shaft into her mouth.

"Open for him, малышка," Sergei said as he pushed upward into her. "Open your mouth and take him."

* * *

Rune's body was on fire. She had been dreaming of the night before. She didn't think anything could surpass what the men had done to her but she was wrong. She could feel the heat pooling low between her legs the moment Sergei wrapped his arm around her. She didn't know what to expect after last night. She was deliciously sore, but would never complain as the feelings Sergei created deep inside her filled her with a pleasure she had never experienced until the previous night.

Rune gasped when she felt a sharp hand to her ass. "I said open and take him," Sergei demanded roughly.

Rune looked up into Dimitri's glittering eyes before her eyes dipped lower. His long thick cock pulsed upward. Her mouth watered as she took in the bulbous head. She lifted her left hand off the mattress and threaded her fingers through the dark hair that surrounded his sack before running her hand gently up the length to hold it still.

"Rune, моя любовь," Dimitri groaned out as his hips rocked up toward her. "I need you."

"What does моя любовь mean?" Rune asked as she lowered her head until her breath brushed along the tip of his cock.

"My love," Dimitri gritted out, watching her lick her lips. "You are my love."

"I like that," she whispered just before she opened her mouth and surrounded him with her warmth.

Dimitri's head fell back against the headboard and he gripped the bed covers on either side of him. He swallowed several times before nodding to Sergei who was watching as Rune's head moved back and forth. They both set a rhythm that matched Rune. The slow pace building the pressure inside them until they were both trembling from holding back.

"Sergei," Dimitri choked out. "Make her come. I cannot hold out any longer. Please..." he panted out.

Sergei leaned forward just enough to run his fingers between the sweet folds. Rune shuddered and a low muffled wail escaped her as she climaxed. Her orgasm exploded around Sergei who stroked into her violently three times before his own cry mingled with Rune's.

He saw Dimitri's back arch upward and the muscles in his arms bulged and strained as he held the top of the headboard. His eyes were closed as he shook from the power of his own orgasm.

Rune continued to drink around Dimitri causing him to jerk as his cock became more sensitive with his release. He finally had to cup her face as it became almost painful in the pleasure of her gently lapping.

"Enough, Rune," Dimitri whispered hoarsely. "You are beautiful."

Rune looked up at Dimitri and smiled. Her lips were swollen and rosy from loving him. A heated groan was wrenched from him as he reached down and pulled her up against him. He caught her gasp of surprise as Sergei pulled from her as she was wrapped against Dimitri's hot chest.

"I will get my shower," Sergei said as he climbed off the bed.

Dimitri nodded as he pressed Rune's face against his chest and ran his hand down her hair and along her hip. His eyes showed his appreciation to Sergei for understanding that he needed time alone with Rune. He was overwhelmed with the intense feelings rushing through him and he needed time to come to terms with them.

* * *

Rune sighed as she rested her chin on her hand and looked out the window of the huge office building of the Vasiliev-Mihailov corporate headquarters. They had been in Los Angeles for almost a week. She tried not to think of how fast time was flying by.

Sergei and Dimitri had been in one meeting after another since the morning after their arrival. They took her with them even when she commented it wasn't necessary. She had discovered a flat glass on the wall that came alive when she pressed the little silver wand.

Sergei had called it a television. He had one installed in the office that first day for her. She had been watching it whenever they were in their meetings. She loved the things called movies. She sighed again as tears filled her eyes.

"малышка, what is wrong?" Dimitri asked from behind her.

Rune turned her head, sniffed, shook her head and burst into tears. Dimitri's expression changed to worry as he rushed forward. Rune moved into his arms and buried her face into his neck as sobs shook her.

"Mr. Mihailov, is everything all right?" One of the executive secretaries asked in concern.

"Get Sergei," Dimitri ordered shortly as he held Rune against him. "Hush, little one, everything will be all right. What is it? Tell me and I will fix it."

Rune shook her head and continued to cry softly against his shoulder. She wasn't sure he would understand. She had never seen anything so beautiful, so sensitive or so sad before.

"Dimitri," Sergei's voice called out as he came into the office where Rune had been sequestered most of the day. "What is wrong? Is she hurt? Sick?"

"Rune, малышка, are you sick?" Dimitri asked soothingly. "Are you hurt?

Rune shook her head. She pulled back to look at both men with such sad eyes. Her chin quivered as silent tears coursed down her cheeks causing their panic to build.

"What is it, Rune?" Sergei asked, brushing tenderly at her cheeks. "Did we... did we hurt you this morning?" He asked quietly.

"No," she responded, shaking her head. "He was... he was going to... to... kill himself. He... he didn't think he had anything worth living for anymore."

Dimitri looked confused at Sergei, who continued to brush at the tears running down her face. "Who was going to kill himself?"

"George... George Bailey," she sniffed. "He had given up everything for his family. He gave... his brother and the townspeople everything. He... he was going to... to... jump off the bridge."

"What is she talking about?" Dimitri asked in concern.

"*It's a Wonderful Life*," the secretary said as she set a tray on the low coffee table.

"What?" Sergei asked with a puzzled frown.

"Haven't you ever seen *It's a Wonderful Life* with Jimmy Stewart? He played George Bailey," the secretary replied. "It's one of my favorites. I noticed Rune was watching it earlier."

"You are crying over a movie?" Sergei asked, turning back around to look at Rune.

Rune nodded. "It was on the wall glass. It was so beautiful. A guardian angel came down and showed him just how special he was. Do you think that is why I am here? That I'm supposed to show you both how special you are?"

Dimitri nodded his head toward the door when the secretary looked at Rune with a strange expression. He waited until she closed the door behind her before he answered. He should have realized after the last week how strange everything was to Rune in her life now.

"It is just a movie, Rune," Dimitri said calmly. "It is make-believe."

"But, it seems so real," she said, looking back at the flat screen now silent on the wall. "He had so much pain inside him. How can someone pretend something like that?"

Sergei chuckled and rose. He held his hand out and helped Rune up. He led her over to the couch and sat next to her while Dimitri poured them all a cup of coffee. He made sure he added sugar and cream to Rune's cup before handing it to her.

"We had better explain this to her before we go to the movie that she has been begging us to see," Sergei said as he sat back. "Movies tell stories."

Rune nodded. "We had storytellers in our village. My father was a great storyteller. He would scare all of us when he would retell some of their battles."

"This is a little different," Dimitri added as he sat down on the other side of her.

For the next hour, Sergei and Dimitri explained how movies were made, what actors did and showed her different examples on their computer. It took a while because she had so many questions. It was only when one of the bodyguards reminded them that the movie would be starting soon and they needed to leave that she finally fell silent.

"What is it?" Dimitri asked as he helped her with her sweater.

"The Guardian Angel," Rune said quietly as she buttoned up her sweater. "That is what I am. I look after those in need."

"Rune," Sergei said thickly.

Rune turned sad eyes to him. "When you no longer need me then it will be time for me to go," she whispered.

"Since that will never happen, you will always be here," Dimitri said forcefully. "Let's go."

Rune walked alongside Dimitri as he wrapped his arm around her waist. In her heart, she knew that her time would soon come to an end. While Dimitri murmured his love for her, Sergei had never once told her that he loved her. She doubted that Dimitri truly loved her. She had only been in their lives for a short time. It was impractical to believe he could have fallen in love with her in such a short time.

She knew she wouldn't want to stay if she couldn't have both their loves. It would tear her apart to lose one of them to another woman. No, it was best that she leave so they could have a chance of finding another they could both love. She absently rubbed her hand over her heart. It hurt when she thought of them with another woman but she knew she had to accept that she was there for just a brief moment in their lives.

Like the Guardian Angel that helped George Bailey, she thought sadly.

Chapter 17

Rune's face glowed later that evening as they stepped out of the movie theater. It had been even better than the movies she had been watching on the wall glass. Dimitri and Sergei had bought her a popcorn and soda. She loved the popcorn, but the soda made her have the hiccups.

She shivered in the crisp night air as they waited for the limousine. Three of their bodyguards stood at a respectable distance, scanning the movie goers that stopped to gawk at them. She turned and grinned up at Sergei.

"That was incredible!" She breathed out. "It was so big and the noise made me feel like I was a part of it."

"We could tell. I have never seen anyone jump so much in my life during a movie," Dimitri laughed as she turned to stick her tongue out at him.

"Don't forget the shouting," Sergei added with a grin.

"I...," she started to tell him she had not been shouting when the figure of a teenage boy near the corner of the building held up a shiny metal weapon similar to what had been in the movie. "Look out!" She cried out.

Everything happened in a blur as she stepped in front of Sergei at the same time as she pushed Dimitri to the side. The loud sound of popping was followed by screams as people began to run, adding to the confusion.

Dimitri yelled out to the bodyguards at the same time as the limousine pulled up. He jerked open the door and pushed Sergei and Rune into it before he dove in on top of them. The driver pulled out and accelerated away from the danger as two additional vehicles that were part of their security detail closed in front and behind them.

"The other men!" Rune cried out in a muffled voice. She was sandwiched between Sergei and Dimitri on the floorboard of the vehicle. "What about the other men?"

"They are fine," Dimitri growled out. "They have the shooter down."

"How do you know?" Rune asked with a grunt as Dimitri pulled himself onto the seat. "Sergei, are you alright?"

"Except for having Dimitri practically throw me out the other side of the limousine, I'm fine," he bit out. "You can let me up now, Rune."

"Oh! Sorry," she said, wincing as she pushed herself up and into the seat across from Dimitri.

"What the hell was that?" Sergei asked as he sat next to Dimitri.

"You know as much as I do," Dimitri said as he answered his cell phone.

Rune looked back and forth as Dimitri spoke rapidly in Russian. From the look on his face, he wasn't happy with what he was hearing. Sergei bit out a few questions that Dimitri answered with either a grunt or a dark look.

"Well," Sergei asked in Russian. He didn't want Rune to hear what was said until they knew the extent of the threat. "What did they find out?"

"The local law enforcement is there," Dimitri replied in a low tone. "No one else was hurt. It appears to be some kid strung out on drugs. Pierre said he was talking crazy stuff, not making any sense and laughing hysterically when they asked him any questions."

Sergei pulled his cell phone out and called the car in front of the limousine. "Get us to the hotel immediately and make sure it is secure. I do not want a repeat of this."

"Sergei," Dimitri said, looking at the blood coating the hand holding the cell phone. "You are hurt."

Sergei looked at his hand in bewilderment. He ran a mental survey over his body. He didn't hurt anywhere. He looked at Dimitri wondering if he had been hit when Rune spoke up.

"I don't think it is Sergei's blood," she said faintly holding her hand out. Fresh, bright red blood dampened her slender palm. "I... It is mine."

Sergei's loud curse filled the back of the limousine even as he and Dimitri knelt in front of her. She looked at them with wide eyes as they forced her to lie down on the seat. She felt Sergei applying pressure to her side where the blood was spreading under her sweater.

"Tell the driver to get us to the hospital immediately," Sergei said in a hoarse voice.

Rune smiled tenderly up at Sergei. "It isn't that bad," she protested faintly. "It is not my time yet. I still have almost two weeks."

"Hush, малышка," Sergei demanded. "What have you done? You should not have put yourself in front of me."

"You sound like Mother Magdalene," she whispered, closing her eyes against the flashing of the streetlights outside the window that were making her dizzy. "She asked me the same thing the last time I died."

"You will not die," Dimitri snapped out as he pocketed his cell phone. "Do you hear me, Rune? You will not die."

"No, I won't die," she murmured softly. "Not tonight."

* * *

"You'll have to wait out in the waiting room," the older nurse said in a stern voice. "The doctor will meet with you as soon as he is finished evaluating Ms. August."

"We will stay," Sergei said with a dismissive wave of his hand. "She should not be left alone."

Rune thought the nurse did a very good job of not rolling her eyes at the two huge men glaring at her. She had been a little embarrassed when the limousine, escorted by two additional vehicles and two police cars, pulled up in front of the brightly lit entrance. Almost a dozen men jumped out of the assortment of vehicles. Dimitri had gently lifted her out of the limousine and transferred her to a rolling bed that was brought outside.

Three people in colorful clothing pushed her through several sets of doors with Dimitri and Sergei speaking rapidly in a mixture of Russian and English. Rune glanced around as they moved through the corridor. She had never seen so much strange equipment in her life. Finally, one of the women in a colorful green outfit told the men to slow down and tell her what happened in English.

"She was shot!" Sergei snarled in a dangerous voice.

"Sergei," Rune rebuked quietly. "They weren't the ones who shot me. What of the boy? Your men didn't hurt him, did they?"

"She is the one shot and she worries for the man who shot her," Dimitri muttered under his breath. "No, the police have him. He is high on some kind of drugs. The police will transport him to a hospital to be evaluated, I'm sure."

"Not here," Sergei snapped. "I will not have him anywhere near Rune."

"Sergei, he was only a child," Rune said, struggling to sit up on the rolling bed as they wheel her into a small room. "Dimitri said he was under the influence of some type of drug."

"When a boy takes a gun in his hand, he is no longer a child, Rune," Sergei responded angrily. "What do you think you are doing? Lie still!" He ordered, pushing gently down on her shoulder as she tried to sit up again.

"I believe the police officers would like to speak with you," the nurse in the green uniform said, breaking into their heated conversation. "Both of you." She stood next to the bed and looked pointedly at both men. "We need to help Ms. August remove her clothing so the doctor can examine her."

"We have seen her without clothes," Sergei stated pointedly. "We...."

"Out!" Rune gasped as she held her side as she finally sat up so that she could glare at them. "Both of you, out!"

"You heard her. Both of you will have to wait out in the waiting room," the older nurse said again. "The doctor will meet with you as soon as he is finished."

"I...," Sergei started to argue when one of the police officers stuck his head in the room.

"Mr. Vasiliev," the heavy-set police officer wearing a dark blue uniform interrupted. "We need to speak with you and Mr. Mihailov for a few moments."

Dimitri opened his mouth to add to Sergei's protest, but Rune's soft voice drew his attention. She had laid back down against the white sheets and looked very pale and fragile. One of the nurses was carefully cutting her sweater off of her with a large pair of scissors. His eyes went to the blood staining the pristine sheets.

"Please," she whispered before closing her eyes. "Go. I will be fine. They will tend my wounds and I will rejoin you shortly. Please, for me," she added, opening pain filled eyes and looking pleadingly at him.

Dimitri swallowed and nodded. Even Sergei had stopped arguing at the pain reflected in her voice and eyes. Dimitri walked over and bent to brush a kiss across her forehead. Sergei stepped up after Dimitri turned and stepped out of the room.

"You will not die," he whispered softly before brushing a kiss over her lips. "Promise me that you will not disappear while we are gone."

"I promise," she said, looking up at him with a reassuring smile. "I'll be with you before you know it."

"You'd better," he responded gruffly before straightening and looking with a dangerous glare at the nurses. "You will keep her safe. If anything happens," he warned in a low voice. "I will hold each of you personally responsible."

"Well," the older nurse said with a huff after Sergei walked out the door. "Isn't he a load of fun? I'll go get the doctor, Judy. Can you and Pam handle this?"

"As long as Mr. Hot and Heavy and Mr. Dark and Dangerous don't come back in," Judy joked as she moved over to the side of the bed.

"Yeah," Pam comment with a sardonic grin. "I didn't think they were ever going to leave. So," she added with a twinkle in her eye. "Both have seen you without your clothes on?"

Rune looked at the young nurse and smiled before wincing as Judy shifted her to get the rest of her shirt and sweater off of her. She looked ruefully down at the tattered remains of her clothing. She lay still and breathed through the pain radiating out from her side. She had been hurt a few times as a young girl. She fought back a shudder when she thought of how her mother had stitched up her leg once when she had fallen on the sharp rocks near the fjord. She had been very careful ever since, not wanting to have to go through that pain again.

"How many?" She whispered through gritted teeth.

She was suddenly very, very cold. The shivers that had started a few minutes ago had multiplied until she was amazed the whole bed wasn't shaking along with her. Her jaw hurt from keeping her teeth from chattering.

"How many times have they seen you without your clothes?" Pam teasingly asked.

Judy laid several blankets over Rune. "If you are still cold, let us know and we can add more blankets for you," she said.

"Nay, how many stitches will you be putting in my side?" Rune asked huskily.

Pam tilted her and looked at the deep one inch gash. "If I had to guess, at least ten," she said looking over at Judy. "What do you think?"

Judy walked around the bed and glanced at the wound. "At least, maybe fifteen."

"Dritt!" *Shit!* Rune murmured, staring up at the ceiling. A silent tear escaped from the corner of her eye to run down the side of her face. "Can I... will you at least give me spirits to dull the pain. I'll need a sturdy stick as well."

"I can understand the booze. I'd need a couple of bottles if someone tried to shoot me," Judy commented good-naturedly. "But why a sturdy stick?"

"I'd need both to deal with those two," Pam responded with a chuckle. "I'd be a basket case if I had the two of them in my bed," she added pretending to fan herself.

Rune looked at Judy with a scared look. "The last time my mother stitched my leg it took my father and three warriors to hold me down. The pain was fierce. Mother gave me spirits after she finished until I passed out. She wouldn't let me have any before as she wanted to make sure I had not done further damage."

Judy stopped pulling items out of the cabinet on the wall to stare at Rune in disbelief. When she realized that Rune was telling her the truth, she shook her head. She looked at Pam, who was staring at her with a raised eyebrow.

"You won't feel a thing after the first pinch," Judy assured her. "Let me see if the doctor is ready. You'll be fine. The doctor will numb the area before he does anything and we'll give you some medication for the pain."

"You go see if Dr. Sullivan is ready," Pam said. "I'll get the rest of the items ready."

"Thanks," Judy replied before she patted Rune's hand. "You'll love Dr. Sullivan. He is a sweetheart."

Rune watched Judy walk out the door. She turned her head and watched Pam in silence as she finished placing items on a metal rolling tray. Pam smiled encouragingly at her as she rolled it up next to the bed.

"So you and Sergei Vasiliev and his bodyguard are an item?" Pam asked curiously.

"His bodyguard?" Rune asked, puzzled.

"The huge guy that was in here," Pam said.

Rune frowned for a moment before she realized that Pam thought Dimitri was just Sergei's bodyguard. She smiled her thanks when Pam added another blanket to her feet. Dimitri had taken her shoes off in the limousine after they made her lay down and the room she was in was freezing.

"Dimitri is not just Sergei's bodyguard. He is the Mihailov, in Vasiliev-Mihailov," Rune said. "He is like Sergei's older brother."

"Wow!" Pam whispered in surprise. "Brothers. That must be something. I'm surprised. I never saw a photo of him and Ms. Ferguson together. It was always Vasiliev and her in the gossip mags."

"Ms. Ferguson?" Rune asked in confusion. "Who is she?"

"You don't know about Eloise Ferguson? The model and actress he was hot and heavy into just a couple weeks ago?" Pam asked. "They were practically engaged until she lost the baby. The magazines say she and Vasiliev were devastated about it. Supposedly, Ferguson was so upset she called off their engagement and retreated. I sure hope he didn't pick you up on the rebound. I had that happen and it sucks," Pam added.

"Baby?" Rune whispered. "Rebound?"

"Yeah. I sure hope he doesn't dump you the way my ex did," Pam said with a heavy sigh. "My last boyfriend didn't tell me until three months later that he had broken up with his wife. What he also forgot to say was that he was still married and they were trying to work things out. Three and a half months later, he dumped me and went back to her. I guess he had really wanted kids and she didn't at the time."

"What... what happened?" Rune asked with a sinking feeling in her stomach.

"With my ex-boyfriend and his wife? They are expecting any day," Pam replied with a shrug. "Live and learn. Take my advice; never ever get with a guy on the rebound. They always go back to the woman the moment she flutters her eyelashes."

Rune opened her mouth to deny it, but an older man in his late fifties walked into the room followed by Judy. He spoke briefly with Pam before glancing at the paperwork she had handed him. His eyes glanced up a few times before he nodded and spoke.

"My name is Dr. Sullivan. So, young lady," he said cheerfully. "Do you think you are superhuman or something?"

"Superhuman?" Rune asked, confused. "No, my name is Rune. Rune August."

Dr. Sullivan chuckled. "I heard you tried to stop a speeding bullet," he said with a gleam in his eye. He shook his head when she continued to look at him with a blank expression. "I guess my age is showing. They must not have made a movie of her yet."

"Movies!" Rune grinned suddenly understanding what he was talking about. "I like movies. That is where we were when a boy shot me."

"Well, let's see what kind of damage he did," Dr. Sullivan said with another chuckle. "Not too bad. A couple of stitches and you should be right as rain."

Rune silently nodded as she watched him wash his hands, dry them, then put on a pair of bright blue gloves. She winced when he touched the area around the wound. A moment later, her side went numb. She clenched her fists when he had her roll onto her right side. He stood over her with a bright light shining down and began stitching the wound. She could feel the tug as he worked on her, but there was no pain.

"'Tis a miracle," she murmured in relief.

Rune smiled up at the old healer as he looked over the rim of a pair of unusual glasses that made his eyes look huge. He smiled down at her briefly before he finished stitching her side. Picking up a pair of tiny scissors, he clipped the end.

"Pam and Judy will finish taking care of you," Dr. Sullivan explained. "You'll need to be seen by your regular physician in ten days to have the stitches removed. If you have any heat, redness or inflammation around the area, contact him or her immediately. You'll need to try to keep the area dry as well for the first few days. Do you have any other questions?"

Rune listened carefully as she rolled onto her back. "No, but I thank you for making this painless for me," she said.

Dr. Sullivan smiled cheerfully and laughed. "I always do what I can. I'll write you a prescription for some light pain medication. You can take an over the counter pain-reliever if you have any other discomfort after a day or two."

"Thank you for your help," Rune said not knowing what else to say.

She didn't understand half of what he was talking about with seeing her doctor or over the counter pain medication. She was just thankful no one else had been hurt and her wounds had been minor. Unfortunately, the pain from her side had moved to her heart. She knew for certain now that there was no hope of her staying with Dimitri and Sergei. She now understood why Sergei had never told her that he loved her. His heart belonged to someone else, even if he would not admit it.

Chapter 18

"She is sleeping," Dimitri said with a deep sigh as he closed the door to the bedroom. "The pain medication made her sleepy."

"What happened, Dimitri?" Sergei said running his hand through his thick black hair. "I find it hard to believe that we just happened to be in the wrong place at the wrong time."

"I am working on it," Dimitri said heavily. "I have assigned Alex and Pierre to find out everything they can about the kid."

Sergei walked over to the bar and poured a drink for him and Dimitri. He turned and handed the dark amber liquor to Dimitri before he sat down on the long couch. They were missing something. His gut was telling him it was more than just a random shooting. His mind went through all the possibilities.

He honestly didn't think it had anything to do with the reason they had first come to Los Angeles. They had the programmer who was leaking the information. It had been easy once they completed their internal audit on emails. The man was sinking in debt and one of their rival companies had offered him a substantial down payment with the promise of additional funds if he could get the latest program they were developing to them by the first of the year.

"I want to return to Moscow," Sergei said suddenly. "Something isn't right. I can feel it. I want Rune where we can protect her better."

"Me too," Dimitri said, staring moodily into his drink. "Pierre said the kid kept saying the old woman told him to kill her."

Sergei scowled. "What old woman? That makes absolutely no sense."

Dimitri took a sip of his brandy and leaned back. "I never said it did. Neither one of us know any old women who would want to kill us and Pierre said the boy insisted he was just supposed to shoot Rune."

"Did the boy say her name?" Sergei asked sharply.

Dimitri shook his head. "No, he insisted that the old woman told him to just kill the girl with you. As far as I'm concerned, it is impossible for anyone to know about Rune. Hell, she has only been in our lives a little over a week."

"It feels like much longer," Sergei admitted as he finished off his drink and stared blankly at the empty glass.

"When are you going to admit you love her?" Dimitri asked.

Sergei threw Dimitri a heated look. "I care about her. That is not the same as love. You know how I feel about that," he bit out evasively.

"She is not Eloise," Dimitri stubbornly pointed out.

"She could never be like Eloise," Sergei admitted.

* * *

Rune leaned back against the door that she had just closed. She had woken up thirsty and lonely and wanted to curl up in the other room near Dimitri and Sergei instead of being in the large, cold bed all alone.

Tonight's events had shown her just how precious her time with them was. Now, she wished she would have stayed in bed. The medication had taken care of the pain in her side but she didn't think anything would help with the pain in her heart.

She had discarded what the young nurse had said about Sergei. There was no way he could make love to her the way he did and care about another woman. Now, she wasn't so sure. She had frozen with the door cracked when she heard Dimitri ask Sergei if he loved her. His comment that he cared for her but she would never be like Eloise seared through her heart.

She pushed away from the door and walked silently into the bathroom. She used one of the glasses next to the sink to fill it with tap water. Sipping it, she looked at her reflection in the mirror. Her hair was a tangle of curls that hung half way down her back now instead of to her waist. Her brown eyes were slightly glazed from the medication that Dimitri had insisted she take as soon as it arrived from the pharmacy. She was wearing one of Sergei's dress shirts instead of one of the nightgowns they had purchased for her. Sergei had suggested it would be better as it wouldn't brush against her side. By the time the medicine kicked in, she didn't care what she was wearing or not wearing.

"What are you doing up?" Sergei's husky voice asked from the doorway to the bathroom.

"What?!" Rune gasped, turning around so quickly her head spun.

Sergei caught her in his arms as she swayed. Rune placed a hand on his chest and another to her head as the room swirled around her. She gasped as she found herself lifted into a pair of strong arms.

"Sergei," she protested.

"You should not be up without one of us with you," he gritted out as he carried her back to the bed. "You have been shot! You've lost a lot of blood, had a traumatic experience and are taking medication which can cause you to be lightheaded. You should have called one of us if you wished for something to drink."

Rune laid her head against his shoulder and sighed. "I can get a drink without fainting," she retorted softly as he gently laid her down on the bed. "Though, I have to admit the medicine does make my head feel a bit light."

Dimitri chuckled as he came in. "You are not used to such things," he commented as he pulled his shirt over his head. "I will get my shower while you hold her. She needs someone to watch over her."

Sergei pulled the covers over Rune before lying down next to her. He tenderly brushed her hair back from her face as she rolled onto her right side to look at him. Rune reached up and touched the line along his brow.

"If you keep frowning you are going to have a wrinkle there," she murmured. "My mother used to tell my father that all the time."

"What happened to you? The first time when you..." Sergei's voice faded on the last word.

"When I died?" She finished.

Sergei nodded as he relaxed next to her. His thumb continued to caress her cheek as they lay facing each other. Rune closed her eyes briefly before opening them again. Her lips curved into a small, sad smile as she remembered her family.

"There was my mother, father, two older sisters, my younger brother and I in my immediate family. It was the end of the summer months and we were working hard to prepare for the coming winter. My brother, Olaf, was one and ten years of age. He was spending more time with my father by this time. They were helping the freed thralls who were under my father. My mother did not believe in slaves much to my father's frustrations. Each time he returned with one, she would declare them free and give them the option of staying and becoming a part of our family or returning from where they were bought. Father finally gave up. Most of those who he brought home stayed and declared loyalty to my parents," she said with a sigh.

"How many were there?" He asked curiously.

"We had close to twenty living on our farm. My father was a warrior under Jarl Bjarni Asvaldsson. He had saved the Jarl's life on several occasions and was gifted land of his own. In addition, my mother was the youngest sister of Bjarni. She and my father fell in love and our family was born. The match between my parents didn't hurt my father's standing. He had been strong before, but now he was also very powerful. Some were jealous of my father's position; jealous and afraid. Over the years as we grew, my father also became very adept at growing crops that were bountiful and was skilled at breeding many fine horses. This made him very wealthy as well."

"Power and wealth can be seen as a threat to many who do not have it or who crave it," Sergei murmured as he leaned forward and pressed a kiss to her forehead.

"Yes," Rune responded with a sigh. "Our land bordered that of Jarl Leifsson, a rival chieftain who was jealous of my uncle and father. Leifsson wanted not only the land that my father owned, he also wanted my father to declare his loyalty to him. Leifsson wanted to rule over the other Jarls, but he did not have the support or power he needed without my uncle and father backing him. He wished to join our families through a hand-fasting between his oldest son, Gamli and I. Aesa was already promised to Jorundr Hasteinson and Dalla was already hand-fasted to a warrior who was away. Father refused all of his requests, of course. Soon after, nightly raids began and two of the freed thralls living with us were found dead and many of our sheep and horses taken. Father approached Jarl Leifsson who swore that it was not done by him or his people. Father knew he had done it, but without proof my uncle would not strike against him."

"But your father did," Sergei guessed.

"Yes. Father and ten of the warriors who lived on the farm set up a trap. Jarl Leifsson's youngest son, Frodi, and four raiders were killed when they tried to burn the huts of some of the families and steal a prized stallion father had raised. Jarl Leifsson refused to believe my father when he delivered Frodi and the other men back to him. He and his oldest son, Gamli, attacked my father," she whispered.

"Was your father killed?" Sergei asked as Rune fell silent for several minutes.

"What?" She asked, distracted by her memories. "No. No, he was not killed them, but he was badly wounded," Rune replied with a soft sigh and rolled over onto her back to stare blindly up at the ceiling. "He made it home with an arrow in his shoulder and thigh. He caught fever and mother nursed him as best she could. She insisted that my sisters, brother and I should go to stay with our uncle. She feared that Jarl Leifsson would take us to force my father to agree. We all argued with her that we should stay and fight or at least send word to our uncle for assistance, but she would hear no more of it," her voice grew fainter as the memories came. "Five of my father's warriors were to escort us. We had not traveled more than a few miles from our home when smoke rose high in the air. We knew that Jarl Leifsson, Gamli and their warriors were attacking."

"Rune," Sergei whispered soothingly as he wiped the tears that escaped as her memories of that day flooded her. "You do not have to tell me anymore."

Rune rolled back over so she could look at him. "I've never told anyone what happened," she whispered. "I would like someone to know. Someone to realize the injustice done to my family because of greed."

"Then I would be honored to be that person," Sergei replied tenderly.

Rune gave a small smile of thanks before the smile died. "Olaf pulled the small sword my father had given him and turned back, ignoring Aesa's demand that he stay with us. I... I told the guards to escort Aesa and Dalla while I went after Olaf," she said quietly. "They did not listen. We crested the rise above our home in time to see Gamli take my father's head from his body. My mother in her grief broke free and attacked Jarl Leifsson. He ran his sword through her before we reached the bottom. One of... one of Leifsson's warriors struck an arrow through Olaf," Rune's voice broke as she remembered watching her younger brother fall from his horse. "He was dead before he hit the ground." She looked at Sergei. "He died a warrior with a sword in his hand," she added tightly.

"What happened next?" Sergei asked reluctantly, knowing deep down he was not going to like what he was about to hear.

"Jarl Leifsson had brought most of his warriors even though he knew my father was still recovering from his wounds. I was able to kill six of his men with my arrows before we were captured," she said in an emotionless voice. "One by one, he ordered each of those who refused to declare loyalty to him killed. It did not matter whether it be man, woman or child. Soon, there were none but my sisters and I. I swore I would kill every one of them," she replied. "I was my father's daughter. He often said I should have been a boy. I gave great insult to Jarl Leifsson and Gamli, challenging their honor and male abilities."

Sergei's swift inhale of breath told her he realized the extent of insult that would be to a Viking warrior. Rune could tell he was remembering the first time they met and how she had fought against both him and Dimitri. She tenderly brushed her thumb over the crease in his brow.

"Rune," Sergei started hoarsely.

"Nay, neither had the chance to rape me as you know," she said. "We would never let such an indignity befall us. My sisters and I struck at the same time. Aesa and Dalla buried the knives they carried in those guarding them before they were struck down while I..." Rune closed her eyes. "I buried mine in Gamli's throat. We were supposed to take our own lives but our hatred for the loss of our family was so great we sought revenge first. My sisters fought savagely before Leifsson's men cut them down."

"Leifsson?" Sergei whispered.

"He lost both of his sons to my family," Rune replied. "In his rage, he drove his sword through me. I remember feeling the rain as it fell upon me. It made me think that even the Gods wept in sorrow for the deaths of so many. Leifsson left me in the mud surrounded by my family. I saw one of the warriors carry the body of my brother and toss it between my sisters and myself. As I lay dying in the mud, I heard Leifsson cursed me to eternal life. He swore that I would remember his rage each time that I lived and died. I did not understand what he was saying at first. It was I who should have been angry yet all I felt was sorrow as I looked into Olaf's sightless eyes. My tears mingled with the rain that fell upon my face," she whispered. "So many lives lost for the greed of one man. He had lost his two sons, I had lost everything. All I asked for was to find someone to love and have a family like my parents while all he wanted was power. In his rage, Leifsson begged the Gods to grant his wish."

"It was granted," Sergei stated quietly.

"Yes, it was granted," she whispered. "I did not understand what was happening at first. I thought I had simply dreamed of my death. I returned the first time on the anniversary of my family's death. I walked among the fields and came upon Jarl Leifsson's holding. I did not realize it at first. An illness had swept through the holding. Many of those inside had already perished or were very ill. I came upon a young woman and child. She begged me to help them. I couldn't refuse. I didn't realize it was Jarl Leifsson's remaining daughter and grandson. Jensina had joined with Jorundr Hasteinson, Aesa's... Aesa's intended, though I didn't know that until the very end."

"What happened when Leifsson saw you?" Sergei asked.

"He wasn't there when I arrived," she said. "He and the majority of the warriors were gone. For three weeks, I nursed those that lived back to health. I did not understand why I was not taken ill, but I thanked the Gods for that fact and the skills taught to me by my mother. It was the beginning of the fourth week when the horns sounded the return of the warriors. By then, only thirty people out of the more than one hundred that had lived in the holding still lived," she said sadly. "The grief among those that lived hung thick in the air."

"What happened with Leifsson arrived?" Sergei said.

Rune looked at Sergei. "Word had already spread of the devastation to the holdings. Many of the returning warriors lost their entire families. When Leifsson rode in, I realized where I was. Rage unlike anything I ever felt rose up. I had saved the lives of not only the daughter and grandson of the man who murdered my family, but the remaining family members of those who helped him," she bit out in grief. "I thought the Gods must be laughing at my pain. I stood looking at Leifsson as he approached. He was drawn and haggard looking, a shell of the man from just a year before. I remember the sound of the wind, the birds and the horses. No other made a sound as he approached me."

Rune's eyes rose to where Dimitri was standing near the bathroom door, listening intently to their quiet conversation. She smiled at him and he came forward to lie behind her on the bed. He carefully slid his arm around her. She relaxed back against him as he pressed an encouraging kiss into her shoulder.

"What… what did he say?" Dimitri asked.

"Nothing," she said softly.

"Nothing?" Sergei asked in surprise.

"Nay," Rune said with a tired sigh. "He drove his sword through my heart.

"What?! After you saved his daughter, grandson and his people?" Dimitri asked in shock.

Rune smiled. "It was the second time he would slay me. Only this time, there were those that remembered his curse. Feelings of unrest moved through the holding. Many believed it was his black heart and greed that had brought the devastation to them and their families. That he would kill the woman who would save them did not sit well with the survivors. Jensina rushed forward to catch me but already I was but a ghost among them. I told him before I faded away that his wish had been granted, that the Gods had sent me," she murmured. "I found out nearly a century later that Leifsson took his own life a few days later. While Leifsson was given the gift of death, his curse lived on and I have continued to live and die."

"What happens now?" Dimitri asked in a quiet voice.

"Now," Rune whispered, looking at Sergei who had grown very quiet. "Now, I think the Gods have heard my plea and will grant me my wish."

"What wish is that?" Sergei asked in a calm voice.

Rune paused as she reached out to tenderly trace his hard jaw line. "All I ever wanted was to be loved and have a family," she said softly. "It is time for me to go home."

Chapter 19

Late the next afternoon, Rune looked around the room to make sure she hadn't left anything behind. She picked up the large handbag that Cheri had given her. She was beginning to appreciate carrying one as she opened it to pull out the scarf that the young nurse, Pam, had put in it the night before.

A thin paper covered in colorful images fell out with when she pulled the scarf out. She bent, wincing when the stitches on her side pulled, to pick it up. Unfolding the paper, she saw an image of Sergei and a very beautiful blonde haired woman embracing each other. Her eyes moved to the caption. She slowly read the words under it.

Billionaire, Sergei Vasiliev, and model and actress, Eloise Ferguson, are seen leaving the world premiere of Ferguson's latest movie, Night Moves in Vegas. Reports close to the actress say she is taking a break due to a delicate medical condition. Is that a baby bump we are seeing? A source close to the actress has stated that the actress is pregnant with the billionaire's baby and that plans for wedding bells are in the immediate forecast.

Rune's hand trembled as she looked at the almost half dozen images of Sergei and the beautiful woman holding each other, kissing or smiling at the camera. Well, the woman was smiling. Sergei didn't look like he was too happy.

"Rune, are you ready?" Dimitri asked. "Sergei has already gone downstairs."

"What? Oh, yes. I'm ready," she answered, quickly folding the paper and placing it back into her large handbag. "I'm sorry for taking so long."

Dimitri walked over to where Rune stood and pulled her into his arms. He tilted her head so she was forced to look at him. A low moan was pulled from him as he leaned forward and kissed her with a barely restrained passion.

"You do not ever have to apologize for taking too long," he muttered as he kissed the corner of her mouth. "I would wait forever for you," he replied, pulling back to look down at her with an intense expression.

"I love you, Dimitri," she whispered. "I will never forget what you and Sergei have given me."

"I will make sure you don't," he said tenderly. He grimaced when he pulled his cell phone out of his pocket and saw the name on it. "Sergei is not so patient, I'm afraid. He never has been," he chuckled. "He said to get our asses downstairs now! I think he is afraid I will be making love to you without him."

Rune giggled when Dimitri bent forward and nibbled on her neck. "I would hate for him to feel left out," she said breathlessly when Dimitri moved his hand to cover her breast.

"Personally, I think it is his own damn fault for always being in such a hurry," Dimitri muttered before he growled out in frustration with the cell phone buzzed again. His expression darkened when he saw the message across it.

"What is it?" Rune asked, peeking down at the small device.

U better get down here! If I have to wait so do u!

"What does that mean?" Rune asked, looking up at Dimitri who was grinning.

"He is horny. How are you feeling?" Dimitri asked, looking at her side.

"Creative," Rune responded with a mischievous smile.

She is feeling creative! Dimitri typed out quickly. A moment later he held his phone out to Rune so she would see the response.

Что ебать являются два из вы ждете? What the fuck are you two waiting for then? Came Sergei's impatient answer.

"Let's go," Dimitri said, brushing another heated kiss across Rune's lips. "I can think of a few creative things I would like to try."

A shiver of delight rushed through Rune. She had spent a long time last night thinking. She could let the past go and focus on her future. She might not have long, but she was going to fill every moment she could with the two men who had made her feel more alive in a little over a week than she had in over a century.

* * *

They rode down the elevator in each other's arms. Rune was breathless and trembling with need by the time the doors opened. Dimitri's hair was messed up, his tie was gone and the top three buttons of his shirt were undone from Rune's frantic hands searching to touch him. She hastily shoved his tie into her handbag and stepped out of the elevator.

"At least when you kiss me I forget..." Rune's voice faded as she stared at Sergei.

He was locked in a passionate embrace with the tall, elegant looking woman from the images in her handbag. Rune's eyes narrowed dangerously even as Dimitri muttered a heated curse under his breath. Rune gripped her handbag against her good side and stepped toward the two figures.

She could tell as she got closer that Sergei was not the one doing the embracing. He had his hands on the thin arms while the woman had her hands wrapped around the back of his head. Several photographers were taking pictures of them. Rune stopped next to the woman and tapped her on the shoulder.

The blonde's head slowly turned to stare at Rune with a look of triumph in her eyes. Rune raised her eyebrow and returned the look with a steady one of her own. She waited until the blonde slowly turned to face her with a toss of her colored hair.

"Yes," Eloise Ferguson said with a fake smile.

"He is mine," Rune stated calmly.

"I beg your pardon," Eloise said turning so that the photographers could get her good side.

Rune tilted her head and smiled back. She had met a few women like this one during her time. She made sure that Eloise could see that she was not one to be brushed aside.

"He does not want you," Rune said with distaste. She was determined not to show the other woman her fear that Sergei thought of her as a momentary distraction. "Take yourself away. Sergei, are you ready?" She ignored the way Sergei's eyebrow rose as she turned and walked out the doors.

"Bossy little thing, isn't she?" Dimitri grinned as he walked by Sergei.

Sergei nodded before he looked distastefully down at the perfectly manicured hand that had reached out and grabbed his arm. His cold gaze moved up to Eloise before he raised his hand and two of his bodyguards stepped forward. He brushed the wrinkle from his jacket sleeve.

"Do not ever try anything like that again," he said quietly. "I could destroy your career with a snap of my fingers. I am not one to be used, Eloise."

Eloise paled before she smiled nervously. "Sergei, I love you. Please, just give me another chance. We had something special."

"No," he replied coldly. "You were a convenient distraction for a short period of time. Make sure she does not come near me again," he informed the two bodyguards standing protectively nearby. "And take care of the photographs."

Both men nodded as he turned away. Eloise's furious scream echoed in the empty corridor leading to the underground parking garage. Sergei made a note to have Pierre make sure that Eloise Ferguson never had another 'photo' opportunity with him again.

* * *

"Rune, *малютка*," Sergei groaned as he looked at Rune's stubborn face. "She means nothing to me."

Rune raised her eyebrow and pulled out the paper in her handbag and handed it to him. She waited, watching as his face darkened in distaste and anger. When he looked up at her, she looked pointedly at him.

"I will not be any man's rebound," she told him quietly as she sank back against the seat in the limousine. "If she is the one you love, do not use me as a substitute."

Dimitri didn't bother trying to hide his grin. He looked at Sergei with twinkling eyes. He slid his fingers between Rune's slender ones and pulled her against his side.

"I would never use you as a substitute," Sergei growled. "She was simply a distraction. I broke it off with her several weeks ago."

Rune nodded to the paper crumbled in his hand. "That is not what that says," she said with a wave of her hand. "You were to hand-fast with her! She was expecting your babe."

"She was not," Sergei bit out in frustration. He ran his hand down his face. "She made it up in an effort to trick me into marrying her. I was never in love with her."

"Just like you do not love me? Am I also 'simply a distraction'?" Rune asked angrily. "I told you once before, I am no man's whore. I will not be used as a 'distraction' then cast aside. I am not some impressionable flit of a girl who feels faint because you deem to flutter your eyelashes at me."

"You are not... I don't expect...," Sergei sputtered in outrage. "I do not flutter my eyelashes!" He finally snapped out.

Rune sniffed and turned her head to look out the window. They were pulling up to the gate of the executive airport where they had flown in. She had nothing else to say about the matter. She let him know her feelings. He could make his choice if he wanted her or that other twit, but he was not going to have both.

"Rune," Sergei started to say as the limousine pulled up to the jet.

Rune turned to look at him as the driver opened the door. "You also will not kiss me until you have brushed your teeth!" She said under her breath. "I will not allow your lips to touch mine as long as she is still on them."

Sergei's mouth dropped open as Rune scooted over and smiled up at the driver as he offered his hand to help her up. Dimitri's chuckle filled the interior of the vehicle as he slid out behind her followed by Sergei. They both watched as Rune walked over and climbed the steps to the jet.

"She is everything that we asked for," Dimitri said in Russian. "You were the one who wanted smart. She is very smart."

"Yes," Sergei said sourly. "And you were the one who wanted stubborn!"

"Ah," Dimitri said with a grin. "But you added passionate. Life with her will never be boring."

Sergei sighed as he watched her disappear inside. She was everything they had asked for. Pain filled him at the thought of losing her. He knew he cared about her more than any other woman he had ever met. He wasn't sure if what he felt was love. If he had to guess, he would have to say if he wasn't in love with Rune, he was fast falling into it.

Chapter 20

They were almost half way through the almost thirty hour return trip to Moscow. Both Sergei and Dimitri had worked on several different issues, held additional meetings with their Singapore and Munich staff while Rune had watched movies and read. It was late in the evening when they sat down to a delicious dinner of steak, seafood and fresh steamed vegetables. Rune decided there were several things that she really loved about this century besides Sergei and Dimitri. Some of them were the food, the wall glass that showed pictures, the comfort of travel, and her personal favorite, the bathroom.

"I think I'll go take a shower and lay down for a while," Rune murmured, setting down her wine glass.

"Are you in pain?" Sergei asked, searching her face. "Did you take your pain medication?"

Rune glanced at him and shook her head. "My side is not hurting," she replied. "I do not like to take the medication. It makes my head feel funny," she added, standing up.

"You can take an over-the-counter one," Dimitri suggested. "They are not as strong and will not cause you to have the same reaction."

Rune smiled tenderly down at Dimitri. "I am fine. I am not hurting," she reassured him before brushing a light kiss over his lips. "Finish your wine. I know you both have a lot of work to do. I am just a little tired and will rest for a bit."

"Rune," Sergei said, rising out of his seat and walking over to her when she turned to leave.

She turned back and looked at him with a closed expression. She had meant what she said earlier. She would not accept being his rebound. She may not be able to claim him for long term, but she could for the few days she had left.

"I meant what I said, Sergei," she said quietly looking up at him. "I will not be used or play second to any woman."

Sergei threaded his fingers through her long hair and pulled her closer. He stared intently down into her brown eyes. He felt like he could easily drown in the dark pools of emotion held within them.

"You are such a beautiful woman," he said softly. "You have a strength that I admire. Your compassion for others is endless. You could have turned your back on those who have needed you but you fought for those less fortunate with no thought of the toll it would take on you," he whispered, taking a step closer to her and cupping her chin with his left hand. "I could never use you and you are far too vibrant to ever play second to any other female."

Rune stared up at him with a skeptical look on her face. "You aren't just saying this to get on my good side, are you?" She asked suspiciously.

Dimitri chuckled and rose from his seat. He moved to stand behind her. Bending, he brushed a light kiss along her neck before he looked over her shoulder at Sergei .

"She has been watching far too much television," Dimitri whispered. "Go get your shower. We will be in shortly."

"You will?" Rune asked with a raised eyebrow, staring intently at Sergei. "Or both of you will?"

"Both," Sergei said roughly, pulling her closer. "I meant what I told you before, Rune. We have claimed you."

Rune placed her fingers against his lips when he bent to kiss her. "Just remember, you aren't the only one doing the claiming. And I meant what *I* said. You will not kiss me until you have brushed that 'nasty-ass' woman's mouth from your own," she stated before she turned and walked out of the small dining area.

Sergei's eyes flashed with desire and humor as he watched Rune toss her hair defiantly over her shoulder. A slow smile curled the corner of his mouth as he watched her. Fire ran through him as he thought of taking her from behind. He wanted her.

"That look will get you into trouble, my friend," Dimitri said, looking at Sergei.

"She said she was feeling creative," Sergei murmured under his breath.

Dimitri's eyes flashed hotly at the dark tone in Sergei's voice. His friend was looking for a fight. A passionate, no holds-bar passion-filled fight. Rune had awoken the sleeping dragon inside Sergei.

"You love her," Dimitri stated with a knowing gleam in his eyes.

"Yes," Sergei replied. "Yes, I love her. I don't care what she believes. I will not let her go. She said all she wanted was to be loved and to have a family."

"We will give her both," Dimitri replied with satisfaction.

"Да, мы дадим ей то и другое," *Yes, we will give her both.* Sergei replied. "Starting now."

* * *

Rune leaned her head against the wall of the shower and closed her eyes as the hot water pour over her. She had covered her head in a shower cap to keep her hair dry and she had a waterproof bandage on her side to cover her wound. Judy had slipped a couple into her bag before she was discharged when she asked how she was to take a shower without getting her stitches wet.

"Are you alright?" Sergei asked huskily.

Rune opened her eyes and stared at him. "What are you doing in here? I thought you had meetings or such to do," she replied.

"Someone said I needed to brush my teeth," Sergei responded with a glimmer of amusement in his eyes. "I thought I'd better take care of that if the only woman I want was going to let me kiss her again."

"Am I?" Rune asked softly, studying his face intently. "The only woman you want?"

"Yes," Sergei replied, holding her gaze with his own so that she could see the truth in them.

Rune stared at him for several long moments before a satisfied smile curled her lips. She reached out her damp fingers and ran it along the scar running under his eye down to his lips. She tenderly caressed his lips with her thumb.

"I love you, Sergei," she whispered. "Never have I felt the emotions that I feel for you and for Dimitri. You have the power to break my heart. I am not sure I like that."

"Rune," he whispered. "Finish your shower. I swear I am having a larger one installed so the next time we travel Dimitri and I can join you."

Rune smiled sadly. "I would like that," she said, knowing she wouldn't be around to enjoy it.

She turned off the shower and reached for a towel. She found Sergei had beaten her to it. He gently dried her face and neck before he moved down the rest of her. She watched him in the mirror as he knelt down in front of her. She briefly closed her eyes as a sharp pain of need rushed through her.

"Turn around and I'll dry your back," he said in a low husky voice filled with need.

Rune turned so she was facing the closed shower door. She raised her arms up as he moved up her body and gripped the top of the glass door. Her breath fogged the glass as he continued to dry her.

"Sergei," she moaned softly.

"You saved my life," he murmured as he carefully dried around the bandage on her side. He pressed his lips along the edge of it. "If you had not pushed me to the side, the bullet would have killed me."

"You don't know that," she said quietly.

"Yes, I do. Pierre found it embedded the side of the limousine," Sergei replied as he carefully dried her back. He pulled the damp shower cap from her hair and tossed it next to the sink behind him. "It was in the report he sent to us."

Rune turned to look up into his eyes. "I don't want you to come to me because you feel gratitude, Sergei. I want you to come to me because I am the woman you want."

"You are the woman I care about," Sergei whispered, brushing her hair back before letting his hand slide down her arm. "What I feel for you has nothing to do with gratitude."

"Brush your teeth, Sergei," Rune whispered, reaching up and brushing a kiss along his jaw. "I will be waiting for you in the other room."

Rune took the towel out of his hand and wrapped it around her. She paused at the door to smile back at him. Something had changed in him. She wasn't sure what it was but something was different. She turned back to walk into the bedroom. It was hard to believe they were on a metal flying machine and not back at their home in Moscow. If it had not been for the vibration she could have believed they were on the ground.

She pulled the towel from around her and draped it across the chair. She was leaning over the bed to pull the covers back when she felt a warm hand slide up over the curve of her ass. A smile pulled at her lips.

"Dimitri," she said before looking over her shoulder at the smooth broad chest. "You took a shower?"

Dimitri ran his hand back and forth over the smooth skin. "There is a smaller guest cabin next to this one."

Rune moaned as he ran his hand around her to cup her right breast. The slight roughness of the callouses felt good as he moved his hand across her skin. She bowed her head as he pulled her back against his body.

"How are you feeling?" Dimitri asked quietly. "We will just hold you if you are too tired or hurting."

"I'm hurting," Rune replied with a teasing smile. "But it has nothing to do with being shot. I hurt for you and Sergei." The smile died as her eyes darkened. "I was so frightened I would lose one or both of you."

"Rune," Dimitri moaned as he pulled her around and into his arms. "When I saw the blood on you... never do I want to experience that type of fear again."

Rune stood pressed against him, her bare breasts crushed against his smooth chest. He was wearing only a pair of black sweatpants that hung low on his hips. Her hands moved down until she could slip her fingers under the waistband and run her short nails along the cheeks of his ass.

"Kiss me, Dimitri," Rune whispered. "I want you and Sergei to take away the fear. I need you both to love me like you will never let me go."

"We won't," Sergei said, standing in the doorway. "Dimitri, kiss her. Show her that she belongs to us."

Dimitri cupped Rune's face between his hands and a determined glint darkened his blue eyes. He slowly bent forward until his lips were a hairs-breath from her own. A low moan was pulled from him when Rune squeezed the cheeks of his ass to pull him closer as her eyes dropped to his lips.

"Sometimes I will do what Sergei says when we make love, sometimes he will do what I say. Tonight, I want us both to take you," Dimitri murmured before he captured her lips.

Rune didn't have a chance to ask him what he meant. Her hands gripped him tightly as he pressed her lips apart and kissed her deeply. Their tongues battled for dominance as the fire between them burst into an inferno of need fueled by desire and fear.

She started and a shiver raced through her when she felt another set of arms around her. She pushed down desperately on the sweatpants that Dimitri was wearing at the same time as she pushed back against the front of Sergei. His hard length brushed against her ass and she gasped when he ran his hand over it before lightly smacking it.

"Sergei!" She pulled just far enough away to cry out his name.

"Kiss me, Rune," Sergei said, turning her in his arms. "Kiss me, *мой красивый ангел*."

Rune lifted her face and pressed her lips to his in a fierce, possessive kiss that told him he belonged to her. For as long as she was with them, she would be the only woman they would want, desire or need. She sucked on his tongue the same way she had sucked on his cock. The low groan was answer enough that he remembered the feel of her lips wrapped around him.

"Sergei, she is on fire," Dimitri said running his hands over her ass. "Spread her on the bed. I want to taste her."

"Get her ready for me, Dimitri," Sergei said, looking down into Rune's desire laden eyes. "Tonight she will take us both."

"Sergei," Rune whimpered.

Sergei pulled her away and gently lowered her down onto the king-sized bed. Rune laid back against the pillows, her hair fanning out around her in an erotic picture of aroused wanton desire. Dimitri parted her legs while Sergei climbed beside her, bending over her so he could claim her taut nipple in his mouth. Shockwaves of sensation swept through her as Sergei's hot lips captured her sensitive nipple at the same time as Dimitri's hot mouth covered her mound. A soft cry exploded from her at the double attack on her body.

"Thor pust!" *Thor's breath!* Rune cried out in her own language. "You will kill me with pleasure."

Sergei pulled back and looked down at Dimitri, who was holding Rune's soft lips apart so he could suckle on the small nub of her womanhood. Dimitri glanced up and the look in his eyes promised that she would be screaming much more before he was done. Sergei turned his attention back to Rune's other nipple at the same time as she wound her right hand around his throbbing cock.

"Сын-из сукин!" *Son-of-a-bitch!* Sergei grunted out harshly as she began stroking him in her fisted palm. "Get her ready, Dimitri. She is gripping me and pumping me hard."

Dimitri broke away long enough to growl out his own demands. "Too bad, I am enjoying myself."

Rune thrashed back and forth when he bent down again. Her body trembled as he lapped at her clit. The combination of having two hot mouths pleasuring her while she was stroking Sergei's thick, long length was too much for her. When Dimitri pushed his fingers deep into her slick channel, she exploded with a loud cry.

"Yes!" Rune moaned out as she came hard around Dimitri's fingers and mouth.

Dimitri pulled back and rose from where he had been kneeling between her legs. With one graceful stroke, he aligned his heavy cock with her slick vaginal channel and pushed through the swollen folds until he was buried as deep as he could go. He nodded to Sergei as he rolled so Rune was straddling him.

"Fuck!" Dimitri bit out. "This position has me buried so far inside her I swear I can feel her womb."

"Just fucking wait for me before you start," Sergei cursed out as he reached into the small built-in cabinet next to the bed and pulled out some lubricant. "She is so beautiful, Dimitri."

Dimitri held Rune up just far enough so he could wrap his large hands around breasts, pinching her nipples between his thumb and forefinger. She bowed backwards with a harsh cry as he slowly rocked his hips back and forth. He shook from holding back his own orgasm as he watched her flushed face. Her eyes were closed and her lips were parted just enough that he could see a glimpse of her pearly white teeth. She was panting heavily as he moved in and out of her. Sergei was right. She was absolutely gorgeous.

"You better fucking hurry, Sergei," Dimitri choked out as he felt Rune moving in sync with him. "She is riding me and I feel like I am about to explode."

"Rune, малютка, relax for me," Sergei ordered hoarsely as he stroked lube along his cock before he ran his hand between the crack of her ass. "Do you trust me, little one?"

Rune whimpered, arching backwards toward him. "Sergei," she panted.

"Yes, my Rune," Sergei whispered as he pressed his cock to the tight ring. "Take me," he groaned as he felt the resistance before he slipped in. "Take us both."

Rune groan and panted as a burning pain briefly replaced the pleasure. She was about to protest against the intrusion when Sergei reached around and rubbed her swollen clit at the same time as Dimitri pinched her nipples. The combination of the twin assaults caused her body to explode again. Sergei took advantage of her release to slide all the way into her. He held her hips still and gritted his teeth as he felt her body pulsing around him.

"Dimitri," he said in a strained voice. "I am not going to last long," he warned.

"I want her to come again before we do," Dimitri replied, looking over Rune's shoulder when she collapsed against his chest. "She comes first."

"She's already come three times," Rune's slurred voice said. "I feel so... so... full."

"Kiss me, *дорогая*," Dimitri demanded, cupping her face between his palms. "Kiss me deeply."

Rune stared down into Dimitri's dark blue eyes for several seconds before she sealed her lips over his. It was a good thing she had otherwise everyone on the plane would have heard her loud moan as Sergei gripped her hips and began moving at the same time as Dimitri did. The combination of one moving deeply into her while the other pulled out was overwhelming. The feel of their cocks stroking the sensitive channels of her body and filling her to overflowing pulled harsh whimpers from her as the pressure deep inside her reacted to their possessive claim on her.

She fought as the combined movements became almost painful in their intensity. Pleasure built, but her climax stopped on a precipice, as if her body was waiting for one slight stroke to push her over. That stroke came when Dimitri groaned loudly against her lips as he pushed up deeply into her as he exploded deep inside her. His climax came as Sergei was burying himself into her.

"*дерьмо!*" *Shit!* Sergei yelled as Rune clamped down on him at the same time as he felt Dimitri releasing inside her. "Ah!" He shuddered as he emptied himself into her.

It took several minutes before either he or Dimitri could move. Sergei slowly pulled out of Rune. The sight was so erotic that he felt his spent cock twitch as if it wanted to take her again. Her low moan told him that she felt his reaction. He rose from the bed, leaving her wrapped in Dimitri's arms as he went into the bathroom and cleaned himself before returning with a warm washcloth and towel.

"I think she is already asleep," Dimitri whispered as he stroked her back. "I love her, Sergei. I cannot imagine our lives without her in it."

Sergei tenderly cleaned Rune before pulling the covers over both her and Dimitri. He tossed the towel and washcloth aside before climbing into the bed beside them and pulling Rune into his arms so Dimitri could clean up.

A soft sigh escaped Rune as Sergei wrapped one arm and his leg over her. She immediately rubbed her foot against his before settling back down. He looked over her shoulder at Dimitri, who lay watching them.

"We will not allow her out of it," Sergei murmured, rubbing her hip. "She is ours, Dimitri. I would fight heaven and hell for her."

Dimitri briefly nodded. He slid from the bed and quickly cleaned himself before returning to the bed. He stared down at Rune wrapped tightly in Sergei's arms.

His friend and brother still had not told Rune that he loved her. A fact that was not lost on Dimitri. He could only hope that his friend did not wait too long before he told their beautiful garden angel how much he cared for her. Dimitri knew all too well how hard, but important it was to expose your heart to the possibility of pain. He had done it years before when he found a scrawny ten year old boy hiding behind the trash cans in a back alley. He had gained a family that day.

I hope we can finally have the family we always dreamed about, he thought as he slid into the bed and felt Rune's arms reach out to cuddle him.

Chapter 21

Rune bit impatiently at her lip. The helicopter that brought them from the airport had landed just a few minutes before and Sergei told her that he and Dimitri had a special surprise for her. Sergei had taken the silk handkerchief from his breast pocket and tied it around her eyes. Dimitri chuckled as he picked her up. He insisted on carrying her into the house, saying he didn't want to take a chance of her falling.

"What is the surprise?" Rune asked for the fifth time.

"You will see in just a moment," Sergei teased.

"But, can't you give me just a hint? Is it big or small?" Rune begged. "What is it?"

Dimitri lifted her just high enough to brush a kiss across her lips. "She is an impatient little thing, isn't she?" He asked Sergei with a grin.

"She certainly was last night," Sergei replied with a wicked gleam in his eyes.

Rune blushed brightly against the white handkerchief. "You two are lethal," she muttered. "Who could blame me?"

Husky masculine laughter filled the chilly air. Rune tilted her head, absorbing the beautiful sound. Her heart was filled to overflowing with love for these two men. Perhaps this is why she was given this last time, to have the chance to experience love. She pushed aside the overwhelming sadness that threatened to engulf her at the thought that she would only have a tiny taste of it. Instead, she focused on the beauty of it. Her heart ached that her sisters and brother never had the chance as well. Dalla's marriage had been arranged and Aesa and Jorundr had been more best friends than in love.

She pulled away from her melancholy memories when she felt the warmth from the inside of the house. Dimitri slowly set her on her feet. She stood, biting her lip and trying not to bounce in excitement. She sniffed the air. It smelled of fresh evergreen and spice.

"Can I look now?" She asked impatiently.

Sergei gently untied the handkerchief and removed it. The sound of her gasp echoed in the entryway. Her mouth dropped open and her eyes grew huge as she looked at the changes that had been made during their absence. Brilliant multi-colored lights were everywhere. Her eyes rose as she followed the twinkling evergreen garland up the curved archway. Twin tall, thin Christmas trees stood as festive sentinels leading down the corridor.

"Oh!" She breathed out. "This is... I've never...." Tears filled her eyes as she walked slowly forward. Her hand reached out to touch the silk flowers adorning the Christmas trees. She turned and looked at both men. "This is the most beautiful thing I have ever seen," she whispered, her voice choked with emotion. "Why?"

"We could not help but notice that you had a fascination with all the Christmas decorations," Dimitri said as he walked slowly toward her.

"Not to mention your love of the Christmas specials on the television," Sergei added with a teasing smile. "I have never seen anyone cry over a red-nose reindeer before."

Rune sniffed and wiped the tear from her cheek. "They were being mean to him and calling him names," she sniffed out. "And the monster wasn't a monster at all. He turned out to be their friend and all… and all… the toys…"

Dimitri wrapped his arms around her slender form and held her tightly against him. Sergei stepped closer and ran his hand down over her hair as she sniffed and hid her face in Dimitri's chest. Tenderness swelled inside him as she cried.

"Do you like it?" He asked softly.

Rune pulled her face out of Dimitri's chest and nodded. "No one has ever given me such a beautiful gift. The first time I celebrated Christmas was with the children. I loved their excitement," she said biting her lip. "I wonder…"

"What do you wonder, мое сердце?" Dimitri asked, brushing her hair back from her cheek.

Rune looked up at him. "I wonder if there is Christmas where I will go to when it is time for me to leave," she whispered.

* * *

Rune laughed as she ducked behind a tree. She had talked the men into going outside after she toured the main part of the house. She thanked each of the servants for their wonderful hard work in turning the house into a Christmas dreamland. Dimitri and Sergei had translated most of it for her much to the surprise and delight of the servants.

"You can't hide forever," Dimitri growled.

"Oh yes I can," Rune yelled as she rolled the snow she had scooped up into a ball.

"Dimitri, you take the right. I'll take the left side," Sergei shouted.

"Hey, no fair! You can't team up against me," Rune responded.

"Oh yes, we can, маленький ангел," Sergei called out.

Rune took off for a low wall that surrounded the outside gardens. She only made it half way before she felt a strong pair of arms circle around her, lifting her off her feet. She turned and pushed the snowball she had made in Dimitri's face. Laughing, they both fell into the soft snow. Sergei walked up on them as they rolled until Rune was pinned under Dimitri's larger body.

"Do you give up?" Dimitri growled in a husky voice.

"Never," she responded breathlessly.

Rune looked up into his dark blue eyes that were filled with laughter. She smiled as she wrapped her arms around his neck and pulled him down to kiss his cold lips. He kissed her back with a desperation that heated both of their blood.

"Dimitri," Sergei muttered. "Let's take this inside where it is warmer. I'm freezing my ass off! Someone put snow down the back of my coat and it is cold."

Dimitri slowly broke the kiss with a deep sigh. "I can think of better places to make love to her than in a freezer," he admitted, before he chuckled when Rune's stomach growled loudly. "But, I think we need to feed her first."

"I want to make a snow angel before we go back inside," Rune said suddenly as Dimitri slowly stood up and held his hand out. "I've never made one before. The children used to make them all the time in the garden when it snowed. I loved watching them."

Sergei's throat tightened as he looked down at her. Her hair was spread out around her and he could swear she had a light golden glow around her. She was their angel, their gift and they would never let her go.

"Make your angel," Dimitri murmured. "Then, we will feed you."

Rune smiled up at them before looking up into the pale, gray sky. Thick clouds, full of precipitation, hung overhead promising additional snow before the night was over. Putting her hands by her side and her feet together, she began moving them in sweeping motions back and forth. After ten times, she lifted her hands to the men so they could help her up. Each took one hand and pulled her until she was standing. Sergei lifted her up, careful of her side, and carried her several steps away to the short wall. He set her on top of it so she could look down at the snow angel she had made.

"Oh," she whispered before looking down at the men. "You have to stand up here as well. You need to see this!"

Sergei raised an eyebrow at Dimitri before he shrugged his shoulders and climbed up on the low stone wall. He turned on the narrow ledge and looked down. He heard Dimitri's swift hiss as he drew in a deep breath of chilly air. On the ground before them was a perfect snow angel. Sergei and Dimitri's eyes connected in stunned disbelief before they looked back down at the snow angel Rune had made. Long feathery wings swept out from the slender figure in the snow. The perfect indentation of feathers were clearly visible. The wings spread out almost three meters, far longer than Rune's arms.

"Isn't it beautiful?" She asked with a happy smile as she looked back and forth between them.

"Yes," Sergei whispered hoarsely. "It is... amazing."

Dimitri jumped down off the wall. He reached up and swept Rune off the low wall into his arms. He held her tightly as he turned and walked quickly back to the main house. Rune smiled at Sergei as he strode silently beside them.

"I love the gift you've given me," she said suddenly. "I will always cherish it."

"Stop it, Rune," Dimitri snapped out.

"What?" She asked, startled by his sharp tone.

Dimitri stepped through the door leading into a small reception room. Rune shivered as the wave of warmth hit her after being outside. She gripped his arm as he set her down. She was surprised when he turned her to gaze down at her with a hot, intense stare.

"You act like you are leaving," Dimitri bit out. "You aren't going anywhere!"

"Dimitri," Rune began.

"No! You will listen to me now, Rune," Dimitri said in a hard voice. "You are not going anywhere. Do you understand me? Neither Sergei nor I will let you go."

Rune took a step to the side of them. She stumbled back another step when Sergei stepped closer to Dimitri. His expression was just as hard and unyielding.

"You don't understand," she said in a low voice. "I don't have any choice in the matter."

"Well, this time we are making that choice," Dimitri said through gritted teeth. "This time we say you are not going anywhere."

Rune gazed back and forth between the two uncompromising faces. How did she tell them that she couldn't stay? How could she help them accept that there were some things beyond even their control? She had less than ten days left. Shaking her head, she watched as the thick snowflakes that had hung heavy in the clouds began to fall outside.

"I do not want to spend the time I have with you fighting," she replied. "Let us take each day as the gift it is meant to be. We never know when our time will come. There is no sense getting upset about something we have no control over."

Sergei's mouth tightened before relaxing. "Agreed," he said, ignoring Dimitri's furious look. "Now, I believe your stomach was growling just moments ago. How about dinner?"

Rune bit her lip and cast them a hopeful look. "And a movie?" She asked. "There is a new Christmas special coming on tonight."

Sergei laughed and shot Dimitri a look that told him the topic was not forgotten. Dimitri gave him a brief nod to let him know that he understood they would talk later. For now, it was time to pick their battles if they hoped to win the war.

"We can eat in the den," Dimitri suggested.

"Yes!" Rune said with a happy smile. Dancing between the two men, she looped her arms through theirs. "Can we have popcorn too?"

Both men groaned in despair realizing they should never have introduced her to the treat. She was becoming addicted to the buttery popped corn. Her laughter filled the air at their reaction.

Chapter 22

Sergei carefully climbed from the bed. He had to unwrap Rune's arm and leg from his before he could move. She spread out the moment Dimitri got up. Even with the pillows pressed against her, she lay in utter abandon.

They had discovered if they pressed her between them she was less likely to travel in her sleep. She liked to snuggle against them. She always had her arms and legs entwined with theirs and when she slept, she slept deeply.

Sergei pulled on a pair of dark gray sweatpants. He glanced at the bed and smiled tenderly as Rune rolled over onto her stomach, half on his pillow and half on the one Dimitri had pressed up against her. A light snore echoed in the room. They had done their best to wear her out tonight. She had taken everything they had given her and more.

He walked on silent feet to the door leading into the sitting room. He closed the door quietly behind him so they wouldn't disturb her when they discussed what they had seen earlier. Dimitri stood with a glass of brandy in his hand next to the fireplace, staring moodily into the flames. Walking over to the bar, Sergei poured himself a glass and drained it. He poured another before walking over to the chairs positioned in front of the fireplace.

Sitting, he crossed his feet at the ankles and sipped on his liquor. He didn't say anything. He knew when Dimitri was in this type of mood it was best to wait for his friend to tell him what was on his mind.

"We have to do something," Dimitri murmured in a low voice. "She has to understand that we won't let her go."

"I have been thinking about that," Sergei said thoughtfully. "In all her previous lives, she prevented harm from coming to those she came to help. It is time someone protected her. We will simply keep her here, where she is safe."

Dimitri glanced over at Sergei before releasing a deep sigh and crossing over to sit in the chair next to him. He was still reeling from what he had seen in the snow. He had been shocked by the image. He knew Sergei had felt the same way. Rune had been oblivious to what they were seeing. In her innocence, she just accepted that was what a snow angel would look like.

"How long do you think she will accept us keeping her a virtual prisoner?" Dimitri asked bitterly. "We do not even know for sure her saving your life is why she was here. What if she is here for someone else?"

"Dimitri," Sergei said, sitting forward and resting his elbows on his knees. "Think! She appeared in our home when we were here. The only other person she met before us was Micha. She has only been with us. She was there when the shooter fired on us. According to Pierre's report, I would have been killed and you seriously injured if she had not pushed us out of the way."

Dimitri released a low curse. "Pierre, damn it. He called earlier, but we were outside. I forgot to return his call. I'll have to do it in the morning. He may have more information on who the 'old woman' was that the boy kept rattling on about."

Sergei scowled. "The kid was high on drugs," he said dismissively with a wave of his hand. "I want to make sure it has nothing to do with our traitorous informant."

"It doesn't. I am positive of that from all the reports from the investigation," Dimitri said with confidence. "So, the only plan we have is to keep Rune locked away in the house until we feel confident any threat to her is eliminated?"

Sergei grimaced. "It doesn't sound like much of a plan, but it is the only one I can think of that will guarantee nothing happens," he admitted. "At least until the New Year. She appears to believe that she will not be here that long. If we can keep her safe until the New Year, I feel confident she will remain with us."

"Sounds good to me," Dimitri said tiredly. "How is the other surprise we have for her going?"

"Micha said it is almost finished," Sergei. "The last of the plants arrived today. He said the only thing that needs to be completed are some touch up painting."

"She always talks about her garden," Dimitri murmured. "She will love it."

"I love her so much, Dimitri," Sergei admitted in a hushed voice. "I can't imagine a life without her filling it."

"Then we won't," Dimitri said, standing up. He set his glass down on the small table between the chairs. "We don't leave her alone and we don't let her leave the house until we know she is safe. I am going back to bed, if she hasn't taken up the whole thing."

Sergei chuckled as he stood as well and stretched. "Are you holding her down this time or am I?" He asked.

"I will," Dimitri grinned. "She likes threading her fingers through the hair on your chest."

"Hey, it keeps her hands still," Sergei replied, running his hand over the dark hair coating his chest.

"Yes, but not her feet," Dimitri shot back with a satisfied smile. "You get those as well."

"I'll have to remember that in our next snowball fight," Sergei said ruefully.

Dimitri paused at the door to the bedroom. "I don't remember ever laughing so much as I have in the past two weeks."

"Or feeling so alive," Sergei whispered as he pushed the door open. "How angry do you think she will be if we wake her up again?"

A glimmer of a smile curled Dimitri's lips. "How passionate do you think she will be?"

* * *

Late the next morning, Rune was once again being led blindfolded through the huge former summer palace. She had eaten breakfast with Sergei that morning in the small sunroom off the kitchens. He was teaching her how to speak Russian and she was practicing with him and the servants who chuckled and grinned as she asked them questions. Outside, the snow had stopped and everything was covered in layers of shimmering white.

"You both have given me a beautiful gift already," she protested. "How can you give me anything else?"

"You will see," Sergei told her as he guided her down another corridor.

"Is it much further?" She demanded. "Where is Dimitri? Is he going to be there?"

"I am here, *маленький огонь*," Dimitri replied, coming up behind them. "I would not miss this for the world."

"Я рад, что. Я скучал по тебе на завтрак этим утром," *I'm glad. I missed you at breakfast this morning.* Rune said slowly in Russian.

"Ах, *малышка*. Ты заставляешь меня так счастлива," *Ah, little one. You make me so happy.* Dimitri said, brushing a kiss across her lips when she turned her face toward him. "I love you, my Rune."

"I love you too, Dimitri," she sighed. "I only understood a few of the words, but I'm getting better. Now, can one of you take this damn scarf off my eyes? I want to see what you've done now!"

"Impatient little thing," Sergei chuckled as he slid his hand over her ass. "Perhaps we should remind you of what happens when you are impatient."

Rune shivered. "Sergei," she moaned.

"I want to take her like this," Dimitri whispered in a hushed tone near her ear. "From behind while she is sucking on you, Sergei."

"She is beaut…." Sergei started to say when one of the servants came out of a door leading from one of the lesser sunrooms.

"Простите, господа," *Pardon me, sirs.* The woman muttered in a soft, polite voice.

"Let us go," Dimitri said with a slight frown as he watched the woman hurry down the corridor behind them. He shrugged when she turned the corner. "Let's see if she likes her new gift."

"Just being with you two is gift enough for me," Rune admitted with a smile. "But, if you insist on surprising me again, I'll just have to accept it gracefully."

"Her true nature is beginning to show," Sergei teased as he took her hand and wrapped it around his forearm. "She speaks smooth words before letting us know she enjoys gifts as well."

"Let's see if she likes this one," Dimitri said untying the scarf.

"Oh my," Rune whispered, staring in wonder at the sight in front of her.

The atrium had been restored to its glory days. Brilliant colorful flowers bloomed in abundance while the waterfall along the northwest corner flowed down over the rocks. Large ferns were embedded into rocks and a colorful rainbow formed from the mist of water splashing down as creatively placed lighting gave the impression of natural light.

"You have told us about your garden," Sergei said as he grasped her left hand and pulled her further into the beautiful garden. "We wanted to give you a place where you would feel at home."

"Sergei," she said in awe, looking up at the huge trees that stretched toward the stained-glass ceiling. "This is incredible."

"Micha has been overseeing everything," Dimitri said.

"Micha?" Rune asked, looking around as she walked along the stone path.

"A garden fit for an angel," Micha said, stepping out of a small area of freshly planted ferns.

Rune turned and gave the old man a watery smile. "You have created a paradise, Micha. This is beautiful," she murmured, unable to resist giving the old man a hug and a kiss on the cheek. "Show me what you have done," she said, sliding her arm through his.

Sergei and Dimitri followed Rune and Micha around the huge atrium as Micha described how he had taken details from the history of the palace gardeners and used it to help him recreate the gardens. They stopped several times so he could explain an unusual plant to her or how he was able to create a certain effect. He also explained that all the metal work and fountains had been restored.

"It did not hurt that Мистер Vasiliev and Мистер Mihailov gave me unlimited funds and workmen to complete the task in such a short time. They insisted it be completed by the time you returned home," Micha explained.

Rune glanced over her shoulder and gave both of the men following her a shy smile. She turned back when Micha pointed out several new plants. They were walking on the path that circled back around near the small office Micha used. Rune laughed as Micha told her how the men had a terrible time catching several of the small birds that had escaped as they were being placed in the cage.

Her eyes swept the manicured gardens before pausing on the Christmas Rose. Her smile died as she stumbled to a stop. Her heart skipped a beat when she saw that only three blooms were left. She took a slow, hesitant step forward.

"What is it?" Sergei asked when he saw she had become very pale. "Are you alright?"

Rune didn't respond. Her throat felt like it was swollen. She reached out a trembling hand to touch a delicate petal. She pulled back quickly when it fell off, leaving only two of the beautiful blooms. She took a step back as Micha bent down stiffly and picked up the fallen bloom.

"I keep these for you," Micha said quietly, holding the fading flower out to her.

Rune opened her shaking palm and accepted the gift. She closed her fingers around the petals and held it against her chest. Drawing in a deep breath, she looked up at the beautiful ceiling. Snow had begun to fall again.

"Måtte snøen falle som kronbladene av en blomst før du slår til tårer av gudene som de våke over den mektige krigeren som han kommer hjem," she whispered in her own language. "May the snow fall like the petals of a flower before turning into the tears of the Gods as they watch over the mighty warrior as he returns home."

"Rune," Dimitri said, suddenly concerned as she swayed. "What is it, малышка?"

Rune looked at the crushed petals again before looking up at Dimitri with a smile. She didn't want her last few days shadowed with regret and sorrow. She shook her head and threw her arms around his neck, pressing a kiss to his lips before turning to do the same to Sergei.

"Thank you both for the best gift any girl could ever wish for," she said. "Now, I would like to see those mischievous birds that like to escape."

Micha chuckled. "Originally, there were two large cages now only one remains," he explained as he turned down another path.

The rest of the morning was spent sitting, sipping fresh coffee and listening as Micha shared stories of his days at the palace. Rune sat snuggled up on one of the lounge chairs under a blanket listening to the water and the birds. Her eyes began to droop as she relaxed back against the cushions. The men talked quietly in a mixture of English and Russian and she gave up trying to concentrate on what they were saying. Instead, she just let their husky voices wash over her, soothing her. They had woken her up twice during the night and again early this morning. She finally gave up trying to stay awake and fell into a light sleep.

* * *

Time seemed as if it was suspended. She could feel herself being pulled into a familiar dream world. One that she knew, but was always a little different than before. It was as if she was caught between two worlds - one that was real and one that was make-believe.

She lifted her face to the warmth of the sun with a frown. Where had the sun come from? She thought it was snowing. Opening her eyes, she saw the familiar fields of her homeland in the warm months of summer. Turning, she blinked several times until she could see clearly.

"No!" She cried out softly. "I don't want to leave. Not yet."

"Rune!" A voice called out excitedly.

She twirled around at the sound of her name to see a young boy running toward her. Her breath caught when she recognized Olaf's lanky form. A moment later, strong, thin arms wound around her waist and lifted her off the ground.

"Olaf?" She whispered, touching the long brown hair of her little brother. "What? How?"

She was confused. She had never seen any of her family before that she could remember. She looked around to see if her parents or sisters were there as well.

"You were thinking of me," he said, releasing her. "I could feel you."

"Where are we?" She asked. "Mother, father, Aesa and Dalla?"

"Only mother and father are here," Olaf replied. "Where have you been?"

"I... don't remember," she whispered, frowning as a sense of panic swept through her. "I don't remember!"

"Do you want to see mother and father? Perhaps mother can help you remember," Olaf said.

"No, this isn't real," Rune said, shaking her head as she took a step back. "I saw you die. I saw all of you die."

"Rune," Olaf pleaded, reaching out to her. "It will be alright. Mother can help. Come with me."

"No!" She shook her head back and forth again. "No, I need to... I need to..."

"RUNE!" The echo of twin deep voices pulled at her.

"Come back to us, little one," one of the deep voices pleaded. "Wake up!"

"We will not let you go," the other voice said harshly. "Wake up now!"

Rune jerked as she felt a pair of strong arms grip her and shake her. She reached out briefly to touch Olaf once more as he began to fade. She whispered her regret before letting herself be swept away from her dream.

"Tell mother and father I am sorry," she called out softly. "I should have protected you better."

"Rune!" The voices bit out harshly as she jerked awake.

"Sergei? Dimitri?" She gasped blinking in disorientation as she opened her eyes. "What is it?"

"You were..." Dimitri started to say in a shaky voice as he brushed her hair back from her face with an unsteady hand.

"Where in the hell were you?" Sergei demanded in a harsh voice.

"I...," she looked around the atrium. It was just her, Dimitri and Sergei. "Where is Micha?"

"Rune, answer me," Sergei bit out in a harsh voice, shaking her lightly. "Where were you?"

Rune pushed her hair out of her eyes. "I didn't go anywhere. I fell asleep."

"You were fading," Dimitri said quietly. "We could see right through you. Where did you go?"

Rune's eyes fell to the crushed bloom of the flower laying on top of the thick wool blanket draped over her. A shiver of anticipation swept through her. She reached out and touched one of the soft silky petals.

"Home," she murmured. "I saw my brother, Olaf. He said my parents were there, but I didn't see them." She raised her head to gaze at the two sets of eyes staring intently back at her. "I couldn't remember you for a moment. I couldn't remember anything and I hated it. I didn't want to be there! I want to stay here, with the two of you."

Chapter 23

The next week was filled with laughter, love and a sense of desperation. Rune didn't say anything but she could feel it in both men since the afternoon in the atrium. One or both of them were always with her. She had put her foot down when they insisted on being with her even when she needed to use the privy. She had come close to violence and had even threatened it before they finally gave in to her demands of privacy. There were times she went in the bathroom just so she wouldn't give into the urge to strangle one or both of them when they tried to boss her around. She definitely appreciated the fact that she needed to be strong to deal with two stubborn, opinionated males who believed they knew better than she did what she needed.

It was Christmas Eve and they had been invited to a huge party to celebrate the night. Rune stood before the mirror in a beautiful white gown that clung to her figure. The dress had long sleeves and a scoop neck with a collar that reached up to show off her long neck. The front had some crystals that caused it to glitter when she turned and the light hit them. The skirt of the gown flowed outward in waves of silky material as she moved. She had braided the front her hair around her head, but left the back to hang in a long curtain down her back.

Her hand trembled a little as a sense of expectation swept through her. She knew that tonight was her last night with Dimitri and Sergei and she wanted to make the most of it. She wanted none of them to have any regrets.

"I am so excited about tonight," Rune said, drawing in a deep, steadying breath as she stood in front of the mirror. "How many people are going to be at tonight's party?"

"Too many," Sergei muttered as he adjusted the bow tie of his tuxedo. "Simone and Petre Danshov host one every year."

"Don't you like to go?" Rune asked as she looked at him in the mirror.

Sergei shrugged. "I do not mind going. Simone and Petre are good friends of Dimitri and I. We have just enjoyed having you to ourselves."

"How did you meet them?" Rune asked curiously. "I've heard the name before, but don't remember who they are."

Dimitri smiled as he walked into the room. Rune's eyes darkened at how handsome he looked in the black tuxedo. Her eyes roamed over him hungrily before lifting to meet his knowing look.

"We met Petre when he was eighteen," he said. "He came from a wealthy family here in Moscow and had been kidnapped."

"That is terrible," she whispered. "What happened?"

"Dimitri heard about it," Sergei said. "Word gets around on the streets. I had developed a software program that allowed me to hack into his father's corporate system. I discovered the kidnapping was an inside job."

Dimitri nodded as he stepped up behind Rune. "Using the information Sergei discovered, we were able to locate where Petre had been taken by tapping into the computers the men who kidnapped him were using."

"Did you get him out?" She asked, gazing at Dimitri in the mirror as he slid his hands around her waist.

"Yes," Dimitri murmured, pressing a kiss to her neck. "It was a surprisingly easy task as his kidnappers were not expecting it. We became friends and Petre's father, out of gratitude, backed Sergei and me in our first business."

Sergei grimaced when his cell phone vibrated showing their driver was ready for them. Looking at it, he sighed. He hadn't been kidding when he said that both he and Dimitri were feeling very possessive at the moment. The idea of sharing Rune with anyone was stretching their limits at the moment. Both of them were still terrified to let her out of their sight after the atrium incident. He drew in a deep breath and adjusted his tie once more before nodding to Dimitri and Rune.

"Are you ready?" he asked. "I would like to get tonight over with so we can enjoy a party of our own."

"I know what I want for dessert," Rune said with a cheeky grin as she smacked Dimitri on the ass and licked her lips seductively at Sergei as she walked toward the door. "Want to guess what it is?"

"Ah, little one," Sergei said with fire in his eyes. "You might get dessert early if you are not careful."

Rune giggled and swept through the door as both men reached out for her. She loved it when their eyes held the promise of a night filled with fire. She had to stop quickly when an elderly servant stepped away from the door leading into the bedroom.

"Oh, I'm sorry. I didn't see you," she said, smiling warmly at the maid.

"Min unnskyldninger, ma'am," *My apologies, ma'am*, the woman said softly.

Rune smiled uneasily at the woman again as she turned away. A shiver went down her spine as Sergei slid his hand around her waist and guided her down the long corridor. She glanced over her shoulder once more, but the woman had disappeared. There had been something familiar about her, yet not. Shrugging her shoulders, she listened as the men joked about how Petre and Simone had met. Simone had been living in an abandoned warehouse that Petre had recently purchased and was not too happy about having to find a new home to live in.

Rune listened in wonder as they related the story of how frustrated Petre had been with Simone's attitude when they first met. Her total disregard for his station in life had driven their friend to threaten to strangle Simone on more than one occasion. Simone still considered Petre's wealth more of a burden than a blessing.

"She resents having to have bodyguards with her all the time," Dimitri said as he helped Rune into the limousine. "She is fiercely independent."

..*

The ride to Petre and Simone's went smoothly. Both men talked about different developments going on around the world. They were both relieved to have the situation in Los Angeles finally resolved.

"Pierre has finished his investigation and I've done a damage assessment," Dimitri said, flicking through a small notebook he had pulled from the inside pocket of his jacket. "It is minimal. The information Stanburg Industry received was from the files I had leaked so we would know who was involved. The new software made tracking the information a piece of cake."

"I want Stanburg's companies," Sergei said, looking at the tablet in his hands. "Break him first before we take over. I want to send a message that anyone who fucks with us will be taken out."

"Are you going to kill him?" Rune asked curiously. "My father said some of the traders used to do that if one of their competitors tried to short them or steal their merchandise from them."

Dimitri chuckled as he looked up from his notes. "Unfortunately, the law frowns upon us killing anyone for such an offense."

"But isn't that what 'taken out' means," Rune asked in confusion. "Someone is always killed on the wall glass when they say that."

"In this case, we break them where it hurts," Sergei explained. "For these types of men, money is everything. It gives them a sense of power and a feeling of being above the law."

"But, isn't what you are doing considered the same thing?" She asked, trying to understand the power plays of the modern world.

"Almost," Dimitri chuckled. "We work within the law and only use our wealth or power to break those that would try to steal from us. We are very careful, Rune. We know what it is like to be at the mercy of those who do not care how they use either."

Rune thought for several minutes before she finally nodded. She didn't understand all of it, but at least she understood a little. Her father had said the same thing when he came back from his trips. That was another reason that he had not liked Leifsson. He said the man used his power and the wealth of his clan for his own selfish purposes.

"Have you heard anything else from Pierre about the boy who shot at us?" Sergei inquired as he scanned another report.

"He was following up on a lead and said he would let me know his findings as soon as he could confirm a few things," Dimitri said. "Did you see the report from Ontario? It looks like they have made sufficient advances on the new medical imagining software."

Rune let her mind drift as the two men continued to talk about the different programs and such. She still didn't understand how this 'Internet' thing worked much less the rest of what they were talking about. She leaned forward and watched as the city came into view. It was a beautiful place in many ways and yet there were many places that were just as tired and depressed as there had been during all her other lives.

It did not matter when in history you lived, she thought as she saw a young couple with their two children walk by. The man scooped up the little boy when he fell and started tickling him until the boy squealed with delight, *families and the division between wealth were all the same.*

* * *

"Sergei! Dimitri!" Simone cried out. "Two of my most favorite supporters!"

Dimitri shook his head. "Oh no you don't, Simone," he said with a rueful smile. "The last time I left Sergei alone it cost me a million dollars. What are you supporting now?"

Simone Danshov was a short brunette with an infectious smile. Rune watched as she reached up and gave both Sergei and Dimitri a quick kiss. A low growl drew a giggle from Simone when a tall handsome man in his early thirties came up behind her and wrapped his arms around her. He brushed a kiss over her lips as she tilted her head to look up at him before reaching out and shaking Sergei and Dimitri's hand in greeting.

"She is determined to send every child that has ever lived at St. Agnes to college," Petre laughed. "I have already pledged two million dollars to start the scholarship foundation."

"I remember you," Rune said, staring at Simone. "You used to come out to the garden and read to me."

Simone looked at her with a puzzled expression. "Where you at St. Agnes, too?" She asked with a frown. "What is your name?"

"You were always so quiet. Sister Carmen said you never spoke to anyone but me," Rune whispered. "But, you loved to read to me and tell me about your family. My favorite story was *The Secret Garden*. You cried when Colin's father came back to the garden and found them. I was so worried about you when you didn't come back out to the garden for so long. Sister Theresa said you had surgery to heal the wounds from the accident that had taken your parents. She would wheel you outside after you were well enough so you could read to me again. You knew I enjoyed it."

"How did you know about that? I never read to anyone but..." Simone asked in a hushed voice. "Who are you?"

"Rune," Sergei said quietly in warning.

"Rune? I don't remember anyone by that name except..." Simone's eyes widened for a moment before they filled with confusion.

"Simone, дорогая," Petre said. "We are being rude. Some of our other guests wish to speak with Sergei. Sergei, I have someone I'd like to introduce you to," Petre said moving them further into the elegant room filled with people.

"I believe I will dance with Rune," Dimitri said as he slid his arm around her. "If you will excuse us."

"Petre," Simone whispered, gripping her husband's hand tightly as she watched Dimitri and Rune walked away. "It is impossible." Her eyes moved to Sergei before narrowing in concentration. "Who is she?" Simone demanded in a strained voice.

"She is the woman Dimitri and I love," Sergei murmured quietly before turning away to nod to the man Petre was introducing to him.

Simone's eyes followed Dimitri and Rune as they began to dance. Suspicion darkened her green eyes as she watched Dimitri slowly turn Rune who was trying to follow his steps. It was obvious she had never danced before. Simone let her eyes scan over the figure of the unusual woman who could capture both Dimitri and Sergei's attention.

"*дорогая*, I have seen that look in your eyes before and it usually means trouble," Petre murmured in her ear. "Dimitri and Sergei would never let a woman take advantage of them."

"I know her from somewhere, Petre," Simone muttered. "I know her."

"She said she was at the orphanage with you," Petre said, brushing a stray strand of dark hair back before letting his hand slide along her bare shoulder. "She was one of the other children, yes? Now, enjoy the party you have worked so hard on. There is much funding to be had this night."

Simone absently nodded her head. Her eyes slid over the couple again as they swept by. There had only been six other girls at the orphanage for the short time she had been there. Four had been in their teens and two had been infants that had been adopted just a month after she came there. She had lived at the orphanage for almost a year before her paternal grandmother had been found and agreed to take her. During that time, she had not spoken a word except to the...

"Rune," she whispered in confusion and disbelief.

She turned away when someone touched her arm. She was soon pulled into conversations with her other guests. Her eyes continuously sought the couple throughout the evening, but she soon lost track of them as her and Petre's other guests arrive.

* * *

Rune laughed as Dimitri led her off the dance floor several hours later. "You are enjoying yourself," Sergei commented as he brushed his fingers over Rune's flushed cheek. "You are glowing," he teased with an uneasy laugh.

"I'm sweating!" Rune said with a grin. "I love this dancing."

"You are glowing," Dimitri laughed. He had shed his jacket and tie once the lighted floor and heavy beat had pulled Rune out time and time again. "She is about to wear me out."

"That just means Sergei will have to 'cut a rug' with me," Rune announced with a huge grin. "I heard an older couple say that. Henry is a great dancer. He showed me the Getter Bug."

Neither man corrected Rune's mispronunciation of Jitterbug. Sergei wasn't lying when he said Rune was glowing. It was more than just the way her skin glistened. There was a light golden glow about her that had him worried. The feelings of desperation that he had been feeling over the past week rushed through him like a tidal wave.

"Rune," he whispered reaching out to touch her cheek again. "You are glowing."

Dimitri's eyes narrowed as he noticed what Sergei was talking about. He had thought the faint shimmer around her had been an illusion of the lights from the dance floor. He took a step forward in concern.

"We need to leave," Dimitri said urgently. "I'll get my coat. Sergei, call our driver."

Rune looked down at her skin and saw the faint glow. She looked up at Sergei with frightened eyes. This had never happened to her before.

"Sergei," she whispered unsteadily. "It's time for me to go."

"Yes, Sergei, it is time for her to go," a cold voice said from behind her. "Why don't you introduce me to your new little toy before I help her on her way."

Rune turned, startled. Behind her stood the beautiful blonde from the magazine. She was staring at them with cold, calculating eyes that held a glint of insanity in them.

"Eloise," Sergei grounded out in a cold voice. "What are you doing here?"

"I know who…," Simone's voice died as she came to stand next to Sergei and Rune. She froze when she saw the small handgun in Eloise's hand. "Sergei?"

"You were mine!" Eloise hissed at Sergei before she coldly looked Rune up and down. "Before this little bitch came along."

"Eloise," Sergei said in a low dangerous voice. "Put the handgun down. You do not want to do this."

"You think I don't know what is going on? I've been in your home for the past week watching as that little bitch took what should have been mine," Eloise said waving the gun at Rune. "I've seen how you and that bastard you call a bodyguard have screwed her. I was meant to be your wife!"

"You were the old servant," Rune said as she recognized the narrowed eyes.

"Min unnskyldninger, ma'am" Eloise sneered. "Even Dimitri couldn't tell who I was. You ruined everything. Your stupid investigator finally figured out it was me who paid the drugged up brat to shoot you. I even gave him extra drugs but he missed. He remembered me from one of the movies I had been in once he sobered up," she choked out. "I had to leave. I was ruined. All because you left me," she whispered, ignoring the crowd that she was beginning to attract. "I did everything to make you love me, Sergei."

"You need help, Eloise," Sergei said, reaching out slowly to pull Rune behind him.

"Don't touch her!" Eloise bit out in a wild voice. "You've touched her enough. Now, now it is time for you both to understand you shouldn't have dumped me for her. I'm going to kill her first then you. You should have wanted me, Sergei."

* * *

Dimitri knew something was wrong the moment he reached for his jacket. His cell phone was vibrating violently before it would stop, only to start again. He pulled it free and pressed the connect call to Pierre. He had to hold his other hand over his ear so he could hear what the other man was saying.

"What?" Dimitri demanded again.

"The old woman is Eloise Ferguson. She booked a flight to Moscow the night after the shooting. She hasn't returned," Pierre said. "The kid remembered seeing her in a movie. I found out that she bought the gun from a pawn shop the day of the shooting."

"Do you know where she might be now?" Dimitri asked before turning around and seeing the face of the woman he was asking about. "Never mind," he said, disconnecting the call.

He walked slowly forward at the same time as he heard a scream and several loud shots. His blood froze as the world around him seemed to stop. His eyes widened in fear before tears filled them as he realized he was witnessing something he never believed in... an act of undying love and sacrifice.

Chapter 24

Micha sat in his small office and listened as the clock struck the first sound of midnight. He poured himself a shot glass of vodka and raised it to his lips. His old hand trembled as he looked at the picture of his lovely wife and young son who were killed in the war over fifty years ago on Christmas Day. Tears filled his eyes as he lifted them from the picture to the window of his office. His eyes froze on the Christmas rose.

He set the glass down on the scarred surface of the old desk with a small thud, spilling some of it onto the wood. Rising out of his seat on shaky legs, he moved as if in slow motion. He took his battered cap off the peg by the door before slowly opening it. He walked toward the beautiful plant pausing as a petal fell with each sound of the bell's toll.

"Oh little garden angel," he whispered in a trembling voice and raised his eyes to the stained glass ceiling. "Please, she is needed here. Please, do not take her."

* * *

Rune closed her eyes as the first toll of midnight sounded in the distance. She could feel the petals falling as the last rose bloom fell in time with the chime of the clock. It was time. She opened her eyes and stared at the crazed eyes of the woman in front of her. She would not allow any more of her loved ones to die.

She stepped around Sergei's outstretched arm as Eloise raised the weapon in her hand. All around her, people stood like frozen statues. A sense of calm settled over her as she began to glow even brighter. She heard Simone's scream as Eloise fired at Sergei and her. The bullets ripped through her chest, turning the white to red for a brief moment before disappearing.

"What are you?" Eloise whispered in terror as she dropped her hand to her side in shock.

"I am Rune," Rune said quietly. "I am the daughter of a Viking, the statue that watches over the children of St. Agnes and Sergei and Dimitri's guardian angel."

"Sergei," Dimitri called out hoarsely as he ran up and ripped the gun from Eloise's limp hand. "Are you... Rune," his pain filled cry echoed. "No, маленький огонь. What have you done?"

Rune smiled tenderly at Dimitri as he walked toward her. She turned slightly to gaze at Sergei. A watery smile curled her lips as she begged him to understand. Finally, her gaze moved to Simone, who stood in shock, gazing at her in wonder.

"You were always so brave," Rune murmured. "So kind, even when you were hurting from your own loss."

"It was you," Simone whispered. "When I was hurting. I could feel you, in the garden. Sister Theresa told me I could tell you anything and you would comfort and protect me."

"You just needed someone to listen to you," Rune said, touching Simone's cheek. "You could always see more than the other children."

Simone looked around her with a frown as she noticed that no one else was moving except for the five of them. She looked back at Rune in bewilderment. It was as if time stood still yet she could hear the sound of the clock in the great hall as it counted down the hour.

"How?" Simone asked.

"I don't know," Rune answered truthfully.

She turned her gaze back to Dimitri and Sergei, who were watching her with barely controlled emotions as she stepped closer to them. She gazed at them tenderly, her heart breaking at having to say goodbye to them. Her hand trembled as she touched Dimitri's cheek. A single tear coursed down it. She gently brushed it away with her thumb.

"I love you, Dimitri," she murmured. "Never in all my lives did I expect to understand the true depth of love. I understand now what it means to love someone to the very core of my soul. You have touched mine and I will never forget that. No matter where I go."

"маленький огонь," Dimitri choked out, raising his hands to her face. "Please, don't leave."

"I have to," she whispered brokenly.

Rune reached up and gently kissed his lips before reluctantly letting him go and stepping back. She turned to Sergei, who stood stiffly, his fists tightly clenched at his side. Her face crumpled as she gazed up at his closed expression. He had never said that he loved her. It didn't matter. She knew that he did. He had shown her how much every time he touched her.

"Don't," he began in a low, strained voice. "Don't you dare leave us. You belong here, with us, with… me."

Rune shook her head and laid her fingers gently against his lips. "I love you, Sergei," she sniffed out.

Sergei shuddered and closed his eyes. When he opened them again, gone was the shuttered expression. His eyes were filled with intense desolation.

He wrapped his arms around her and buried his face in the curve of her neck. Rune held him tightly as his body shook violently. She threaded her fingers through his hair and gently cooed as low, choked moans escaped him. She held him until she felt the pull as the last few strokes of the clock rung out.

"Tell me," she begged. "Please, just once. Tell me."

Sergei pulled back and looked at her with eyes filled with agony. He kissed her, the salty taste of his tears mixed with his desperation. His hands cupping her face as he tried to hold onto her.

"I love you," he whispered desperately. "Don't, don't go."

"I love you both," she whispered as the last sounds of the clock began to fade. "I'll never forget you," her voice echoed huskily. "I'll never forget," she said again before she faded away.

"No!" Sergei and Dimitri both yelled at the same time as everyone started moving again.

"Get her!" Petre shouted out as he wrapped his arms around Simone's shaking figure. He turned so his body was between Simone's and Eloise. Several of his security personnel rushed forward to grip Eloise's limp figure. "Get her out of here and call the police. Where is Rune? Sergei? Dimitri? Where is Rune?" He asked looking around frantically.

"She's gone," Simone responded in a dazed voice. "She... she's gone.

Sergei was on his knees on the floor where Rune last stood. Dimitri stood over him with his hand on his shoulder. Scattered all around them were the delicate red petals of the Christmas rose.

* * *

"Runa," Olaf yelled as he ran toward her. "You came back!"

"Olaf," Rune whispered before she collapsed in the green meadow with a low cry.

She felt Olaf's thin arms wrap around her as she knelt in the grass, rocking as she sobbed. She thought there would be no pain in death but she felt like her heart was being ripped from her chest. She gasped as wave after wave of grief threatened to overwhelm her.

"Come with me," Olaf said helping her to stand. "Mother and father will know what to do."

Rune leaned heavily against her younger brother. He seemed taller, stronger than he had in real life. She let him guide her as she was too blinded by tears to see where she was going. All she knew was she wanted the horrible pain sweeping through her to finally take her away.

A small hut soon came into view. Horses, sheep and several dogs stood watching as they approached.

Olaf called out a soft word of warning to the dogs who laid back down. The door to the hut opened and an older version of Rune stood in the doorway drying her hands on an off-white apron.

"Runa," Asta rushed forward and wrapped her arms around her youngest daughter's slender waist. "Oh Runa."

"It hurts, *mor*" Rune whispered. "I love them so much. I can't bear the pain of leaving them."

"Oh child," Asta said soothingly. "Come, tell us about them."

Rune looked up as her mother turned sideways to give her room to enter the hut. Her eyes fell on the huge figure of her father. He didn't say a word, just opened his arms wide for her. She rushed forward needing his strong, steady arms to comfort her.

"*Far*, help me," she begged. "Please, help me return to them."

"We will do everything we can, my Runa," Sven murmured. "Now, dry your tears and tell your mother and I about them."

Rune looked up into the twinkling eyes of her father. A small smile curved her lips and she nodded. She looked around the room for Dalla and Aesa before looking over at Olaf. She turned concerned eyes back to her parents.

"Aesa? Dalla?" She forced out.

"They have not come home yet," Asta said as she set a bowl of stew and fresh bread on the table. "Now, tell us of your wonderful adventures."

Rune slowly nodded and followed her parents and brother over to the long wooden table. Sitting on the bench, she drew in a deep breath, wondering where to begin. She finally decided to start at the beginning.

"I'm sorry I did not keep Olaf, Aesa and Dalla safe," she began. "We were several miles from home when we first saw the smoke…."

Over the next few hours, Rune related each and every life she had lived. Her voice grew soft as she talked about the children of St. Agnes and the nuns there that had touched her heart. The tears did not come again until she told them of her first meeting with Dimitri and Sergei. That was when she knew that she could not go on without them.

Chapter 25

Neither man spoke on the return trip home. Both were locked in their own grief. Petre's security staff was taking care of Eloise. After the shooting, she had just babbled incoherently. It was obvious that she was not well. Personally, neither cared what happened to her.

The limousine pulled up along the front drive and the driver quickly jumped out to open the door for them. Dimitri slid out first. He gave the man a brief nod as he pulled the collar of his jacket further up. His eyes moved upward to scan the dark sky. Brilliant stars glittered down at him and he wondered briefly if Rune was looking down on them. Grief choked him and his eyesight blurred.

"Do you think she...." he choked out, turning to look back at Sergei as he stepped out of the limousine.

"Don't!" Sergei replied sharply. "Don't," he repeated in a thick voice as he strode past Dimitri and up the stairs leading into the house.

Sergei walked down the long hallway, ignoring the servant who was standing by the door waiting to take his jacket. He turned the corner and pushed open the door to the library. A large fire had been started in the fireplace, but even the combined heat of the fire and room heater could do nothing to melt the ice that was closing around his heart. He embraced the icy feeling, hoping it would help keep the pain at bay. He didn't know what he would do when it melted.

Walking over to the bar, he poured a small glass full of the brandy he enjoyed and drained it before pouring another then another. Even the burn of expensive liquor did nothing to ease the building pressure inside him. He turned as Dimitri entered the room.

His face twisted as the realization that Rune would never walk through the door again slammed into him. A low howl of pain and rage burst from him. He turned and threw the glass in his hand violently into the fire before he bowed his head and drew in long, agonizing breaths.

"Why, Dimitri? We should never have taken her out of the house," Sergei said, his voice growing louder as his pain increased. "How could that bitch have slipped through our security? I want all of their heads," he bit out, turning to look at Dimitri with burning eyes. "I want every fucking security members' head, do you hear me?"

Dimitri was having a hard enough time dealing with his own pain and grief. Sergei's demands mirrored the thoughts running through his mind on the long drive from Petre and Simone's home. Anger flared deep inside him and he spoke without thinking when he walked over to the bar near Sergei and poured himself a tall glass of whiskey.

"Maybe you should look at yourself first!" Dimitri gritted out harshly.

"What do you mean by that?" Sergei asked, glaring at Dimitri.

Dimitri turned and stared coldly back at Sergei. "Meaning if you hadn't touched that bitch Ferguson in the first place Rune would still be alive!" He said harshly, regretting the words as soon as they burst from his lips.

"You bastard," Sergei growled, grabbing the front of Dimitri's shirt and shoving him up against the bar. "You think I am to blame for Rune dying? You were supposed to protect her! You were in charge of the security. It was your responsibility to keep her safe!"

Dimitri's glass shattered as it hit the marble floor in front of the bar. He grabbed Sergei's wrists and twisted, turning his friend and wrapping one of his thick arms around his neck. Guilt washed through him as he realized what he was doing. He pushed Sergei away from him and swiveled until he was bent over the bar. His knuckles were white as he gripped the edge of it. His shoulders shook from the force of the pain and guilt flooding him.

"Do you think I don't blame myself?" Dimitri asked thickly. "I should have been there to protect her. I should have been there," he howled as he raised his fists up and slammed them down on the top of the bar with enough force to knock over several glasses. "I should have been the one to take the bullets," he whispered as he bowed his head and cried.

Sergei stood behind his brother. Dimitri had always put him first. When they were young and food was scarce, Dimitri would insist that he be the one to eat. When it was cold and they hadn't more than a blanket to help warm them, Dimitri had always made sure that he had enough to cover him. When the thugs were after them, it was Dimitri who would stand between them and Sergei. He always put Sergei first, just as he had Rune.

Sergei walked over and gently laid his hand on Dimitri's shoulder. "I'm sorry," he said quietly. "I'm sorry, my brother."

Dimitri turned tortured eyes to Sergei. "I don't know why," he choked out. "I don't know why, Sergei. I love her so much."

Sergei's throat closed up, but he knew he had to force the words out. He should have told Rune every second of the day how much he loved her. It had taken losing her to finally open himself to what it meant to love someone to the center of his being.

"I love her too, Dimitri," Sergei confessed. "I love her so much I don't know how to handle the pain inside me."

Dimitri reached out and gripped Sergei's shoulders in understanding. Somehow, someway they would make it. He was not sure how. He knew that in all the trials and challenges they had faced growing up, this one would be the most difficult to survive.

"Come," Dimitri said heavily. "I don't know about you, but I need a drink."

Sergei nodded. He grabbed the decanter of brandy and another glass before walking over to the chair in front of the fire. He shrugged off his jacket and draped it over the back of the chair before he sat down and poured the strong liquor into the glass. He didn't even bother setting the decanter down. He planned on drinking it and several more before the night was over. He glanced at Dimitri who did the same, only he had grabbed the bottle of whiskey not bothering with a glass.

"Where do we go from here?" Sergei asked, staring into the flames.

Dimitri shrugged as he sat down in the other chair. "Right now, I don't want to think of tomorrow. I can't," he added softly before he took a deep swig from the bottle.

* * *

Rune looked around her as she walked through the tall grass of the meadow. She had risen hours before. Her father strode silently beside her as they climbed to the top of the hill that looked out over the vast ocean far below. She stood still. The white gown of the evening dress she had worn to the party clung to her and her hair blew loosely behind her as a light breeze swept up the tall cliff.

Neither spoke as they waited for the sun to rise. On the horizon, the faint light turned the sky into a vivid painting of orange, yellow, pinks and blues. Rune gazed out on the beauty of it, but her heart ached too much to enjoy it.

"What is your wish?" Her father asked her quietly.

"To be with Dimitri and Sergei," Rune responded immediately. She stared straight ahead for several seconds before she turned eyes that glittered with unshed tears up to him. "To make a family with them as their wife," she added before she turned to look back out at the sunrise.

Sven smiled down at his beautiful, brave daughter. She was the image of his wife and just as strong and stubborn. She would need to be if she hoped to handle the two males that he had been listening to throughout the night. He had wanted to know that they would love and protect her. If he was going to send his daughter back to the living, he wanted to make sure that she would be happy and loved.

"I love you, daughter," Sven said, brushing a strand of hair from her face and leaning down to kiss her gently on her cheek. "Your mother and I will watch over you always."

Rune turned puzzled eyes to her father for just a moment before the world tilted under her feet. She cried out, reaching for him to steady her. Her hands swept through his body as she fell from the cliff. She closed her eyes as she continued to fall. A wave of warmth engulfed her when she should have hit the water and darkness descended around her like a velvet blanket.

"Father!" Olaf called out, running up the hill.

Sven turned and looked behind him. He waited as Olaf and Asta joined him. The three of them stood on the edge of the cliff looking down.

"She has returned?" Asta asked.

Sven smiled lovely down at his wife's upturned face and brushed a light kiss against her lips. "Ja," he said, looking back at the sunrise.

Olaf sighed and kicked at a stone. "So, now we just have to wait for Aesa and Dalla? How much longer before they come to visit?" He asked glumly.

"Not long, Olaf," Sven told his son. "Not long. How about a ride along the cliffs? Perhaps we will find them," he asked.

Olaf's face lit up with excitement. "I'll get the horses," he replied before he took off back down the hill at a loping run.

"I will miss him when it is his time to go," Asta said, tears in her eyes as she turned back to watch as Rune slid further away. "Will she be alright?"

"Oh yes," Sven said, wrapping his massive arms around his slender wife. "She is just what those two men need and they are perfect for our Runa."

Asta leaned her head back and smiled. Their life may have been cut short but the Gods worked in mysterious ways. She did not question where they were, she simply accepted that there were some things best left alone. As long as she had Sven, she was content no matter where they were sent. They both turned as Olaf returned riding one of the horses.

"How about riding with us?" Sven asked, looking down.

"Olaf only brought two horses," Asta commented.

Sven laughed as he lifted his wife in his arms. "Since when has that ever stopped us?"

Chapter 26

A hesitant knock on the door woke Sergei. He groaned and massaged his neck as he slowly woke. He looked around noticing he was lying on the couch in the library still. The fire burned low in the grate and there was a chill in the air. A throw blanket fell to his lap as he sat up. He breathed deeply through his nose as he tried to determine if the pounding he was hearing was from his head or the door.

He grimaced when the knock sounded again. He threw off the blanket and stiffly rose. Dimitri was snoring on the rug in front of the fire. He grumbled when the third knock sounded and rolled over, knocking several empty bottles of whiskey over as he turned.

Sergei staggered to the door. It took him several tries and a few curses before his hand found the doorknob. He jerked it open, hanging onto the edge of it as he cast a bleary-eyed glare at whoever had the nerve to interrupt them. His eyes narrowed when he saw Micha nervously standing on the other side of the door, clenching his battered cap between his snarled fingers.

"What is it?" Sergei asked harshly.

"It… it is the statue," Micha whispered nervously.

Sergei frowned and shook his head, trying to clear it enough to understand what Micha was saying. He groaned as the room spun. Clutching his forehead with the hand that was bent against the door while he held on tightly to the doorknob with the other so he wouldn't fall, he blinked blankly at Micha.

"What?" Sergei asked again.

"It's the statue," Micha said. "The garden angel's statue. It is back."

Sergei's mind cleared and he straightened enough to let go of the door and grip the front of Micha's jacket. He shook the old man and glared at him. Speaking over a mouth that felt like it was full of cotton, he had to start over twice before he could get the words out where they made sense.

"What did you say?" Sergei asked in disbelief.

"I said the statue is back," Micha said with a small smile.

"Hold that thought," Sergei said hoarsely as he let go of Micha's jacket and stumbled over to where Dimitri was passed out on the rug. He gave Dimitri a light kick the ribs, knowing he would never be able to bend over and shake him.

Dimitri sat up, looking around wildly before he leaned forward and grabbed his head. "Сын-из сукин!" *Son-of-a-bitch!* He glared up at Sergei. "What?"

"The statue is back," Sergei said. "Rune. Dimitri, the statue… Rune," he repeated incoherently. "Come on!"

He bent and helped Dimitri up. It took several tries and both of them almost ended up face first on the floor before they could stand. He glanced at Micha who stood silently at the door looking at them with a small knowing smile.

"Lead the way," Sergei choked out as he wrapped an arm around Dimitri when the other male's legs started to give out. "Wake up damn it, Dimitri."

"I'm awake, but I feel like shit," Dimitri muttered as he gritted his teeth against the pain in his head. "What the fuck is going on?"

"Micha says Rune's statue is back," Sergei said.

Dimitri's eyes cleared a bit as he looked at the old man. "Rune?"

Micha shook his head. "Just the statue. It appeared just a few moments ago," he said in a shaky voice.

Dimitri shook Sergei's arm off as he rubbed his face. He nodded sharply to Sergei to let him know that he was awake. He wanted to see for himself that the statue had returned.

"What are we waiting for?" He snapped out sharply. "Go!"

* * *

Sergei, Dimitri and Micha walked swiftly down the still dark corridors. It took everything in both men not to burst into a run. Two things prevented that. The first was they were both still suffering from massive hangovers and would have fallen before they took more than a half dozen steps. The second was fear. Fear to hope. Fear to dream. Fear that she would have disappeared by the time they reached the atrium. It was the second that kept them walking slowly behind Micha.

The three entered the atrium and walked down the paths leading to the center platform. Just as Micha had said, the bronze statue of their garden angel stood watch over the gardens they had recreated just for her. Micha stepped to one side. He understood this would be difficult for both men. He muttered quietly that he would be in his office should they need him.

Neither man acknowledged Micha as he walked away. Their eyes were glued to the beautiful statue standing serenely in the center of the raised marble platform. They approached as one, stopping at the bottom so they could drink in Rune's peaceful face. Sergei took a hesitant step up the steps. His fingers trembled violently as he reached out and touched her cheek. Instead of the warmth that he had felt the first time, his fingers touched cold metal.

"Oh, моя прекрасная любовь," *Oh, my beautiful love*, he whispered, drinking in her features. "You have no idea how much I love you. How much I need you. Please, please come back to us. Please, Rune. Please come back to us, my love," he whispered in a broken voice. "Please," he choked out as tears filled his eyes and spilled down his cheeks unnoticed.

Dimitri took a step closer. His throat was frozen as he stared hungrily at the face of the statue. She was gone. He could feel it. Before, he could feel the heat of her stare when she had been a statue before. Now, there was nothing but a beautiful empty replica of their angel.

"She's gone," Dimitri said in a strained voice. "She's..."

A soft moan drew their attention to the metal bench off to the side of the platform. They watched in disbelief as a slender figure slowly sat up and stretched before a pair of dark brown eyes popped open. Familiar lips twisted into a rueful smile as the eyes moved back and forth between them before turning to the nightgown that she was wearing.

"Sometimes he has a really lousy sense of humor," she said softly with a humorous smile curving her lips. "But, I really, really want to be here so I don't mind," she said, standing up, shivering as her bare feet touched the cold ground. "And I really, really love him for sending me back."

"Rune," Sergei choked out.

"I love you too, Sergei," she said, raising her arms to them. "I love you both! I don't ever want to lose you again."

Sergei took a step forward, then two, before he jogged down the steps and wrapped his arms around her. He held her tightly against his body, his face buried in the curve of her shoulder as silent sobs shook his large frame. Rune looked over his shoulder at Dimitri, who stood on the bottom step watching them.

"I love you, Dimitri," Rune whispered tenderly. "I need you. We need you," she added, holding out her hand to him.

Sergei turned, uncaring that his friend and surrogate brother saw the dampness on his face. The look of love, hope and warmth in Dimitri's eyes made Sergei realize the pain his brother had hidden from him. He waited until Dimitri was close enough to touch Rune before he let her go.

"For how long?" Dimitri choked out, standing stiffly.

"For as long as you want me," Rune replied, looking at both men. "Forever if you want."

"I want forever," Dimitri demanded hoarsely. "Sergei and I… we want forever."

"Just remember it goes both ways," she laughed out as she threw her arms around his neck. "You are both mine as well."

"From the moment we touched you, Rune, you have held our hearts," Sergei said pressing a kiss to her neck.

Rune leaned back against Sergei, content to be trapped between the two men. Especially since they were both warm and she was freezing. Her eyes moved upward to the stained glass ceiling of the atrium.

You have a lousy sense of humor, she thought ruefully. *You could have at least given me my robe and slippers.*

A soft chuckle was her only response.

Epilogue

One Year Later

Rune stood in front of the mirror getting ready for the huge Christmas party they were throwing. Their guests would be arriving shortly. So much had changed over the past year. She looked down at the huge diamond ring that glittered on her finger.

Sergei and Dimitri had insisted that they marry immediately. They'd had a small wedding with just close friends before having a larger one for the world. To the world, she was legally married to Sergei but to everyone who knew them, she was married to both men.

Rune's eyes widened when Dimitri reached into his pocket and pulled out a dark sapphire and diamond necklace that matched the dark blue of her evening gown. With her hair swept up, it left her pale throat bare. She watched as he hooked the clasp.

"It's beautiful," she said, fingering the delicate necklace. "You know, I don't need anything else."

"We know that you do not want anything else but it gives us pleasure to be able to give you something," Sergei said as he nodded to Dimitri. "You have given both of us something that we have always wanted, but always thought would be nothing more than a wish."

Rune's eyes softened as she found herself pinned between the two men. Well, pinned as close as Sergei could get to her with her stomach rounded. She gave him a rueful smile as she laid her hand over it.

"Is he moving again?" Sergei asked in a husky voice.

Rune laughed. "He always moves when you two get close to me. I swear he thinks it is play time," she chuckled.

A knock on the door drew their attention. Dimitri reached around her and rubbed the small foot that was pressing outward. He chuckled as their son rolled and Rune's face turned to resignation.

"On the bladder?" He teased as he kissed her neck.

"You laugh now, but don't forget you two promised to get up during the night and bring him to me when he is born," she said. "Privy!" She muttered before hurrying off to the bathroom.

Sergei opened the door and saw one of the servants standing in the doorway. He spoke quietly before he turned to look as Rune came back into the room straightening her gown. He held out his hand to her as she came forward.

"Are the guests arriving?" She asked as she waddled toward him.

"Yes," Dimitri held the door open.

They walked down the long corridor to the entry hall. Their guests were just arriving. Sergei and Dimitri stood on each side of Rune as they greeted their guests before she began to droop.

Simone came to her rescue, leading Rune into one of the main ballrooms and insisting that she rest for a bit. Both women had become best friends over the past year. Simone had burst into tears and thrown her arms around Rune the first time she saw her after learning that she was alive.

They sat talking quietly until Rune's attention was caught by the figure of a slender girl as she glanced around before slipping into one of the side rooms. There was something familiar about her. A moment later, a tall furious male glanced around before his eyes narrowed on the door the girl had disappeared through.

"Who is that?" Rune asked Simone.

"That is Sheik Nasser Al-Rashid," Simone said. "He doesn't look very happy."

"Who is the girl that he is looking for?" Rune asked.

She turned to look back at the door to the small sitting room where the girl had escaped into. There was another door leading out of it. Rune decided if she had someone who looked that angry, looking for her, she would probably use it the first chance she got.

"I think Petre said her name was Dalla something or other. I can remember her last name. I think it started with a 'B'," Simone replied.

Rune's eyes widened before a slow grin curved her lips. Her eyes glowed with speculation. Dalla was an unusual name and the girl reminded her of her older sister. Her eyes swept through the room, stopping on Sergei and Dimitri who were walking toward her. If it was possible for her to return, who was to say it wasn't possible for her sisters to also return.

"Rune, are you alright?" Dimitri asked as he reached her.

"I've never felt better," she replied as her hand rubbed the swell of her stomach. "I think our family might be growing."

To be continued: **Challenging Dalla**

If you loved this story by me (S.E. Smith) please leave a review. You can also take a look at additional books and sign up for my newsletter at **http://sesmithfl.com** to hear about my latest releases or keep in touch using the following links:

Website: http://sesmithfl.com
Newsletter: http://sesmithfl.com/?s=newsletter
Facebook: https://www.facebook.com/se.smith.5
Twitter: https://twitter.com/sesmithfl
Pinterest: http://www.pinterest.com/sesmithfl/
Blog: http://sesmithfl.com/blog/
Forum: http://www.sesmithromance.com/forum/

Excerpts of S.E. Smith Books

If you would like to read more S.E. Smith stories, she recommends Touch of Frost, the first in her Magic, New Mexico series. Or if you prefer Westerns with a twist or Sci-fi, you can check out Indiana Wild or Abducting Abby…

Additional Books by S.E. Smith

Short Stories and Novellas
For the Love of Tia
(Dragon Lords of Valdier Book 4.1)
A Dragonling's Easter
(Dragonlings of Valdier Book 1.1)
A Dragonling's Haunted Halloween
(Dragonlings of Valdier Book 1.2)

A Dragonling's Magical Christmas
    (Dragonlings of Valdier Book 1.3)
A Warrior's Heart
    (Marastin Dow Warriors Book 1.1)
Rescuing Mattie
    (Lords of Kassis: Book 3.1)

Science Fiction/Paranormal Novels

Cosmos' Gateway Series
Tink's Neverland (Cosmos' Gateway: Book 1)
Hannah's Warrior (Cosmos' Gateway: Book 2)
Tansy's Titan (Cosmos' Gateway: Book 3)
Cosmos' Promise (Cosmos' Gateway: Book 4)
Merrick's Maiden (Cosmos' Gateway Book 5)

Curizan Warrior
Ha'ven's Song (Curizan Warrior: Book 1)

Dragon Lords of Valdier
Abducting Abby (Dragon Lords of Valdier: Book 1)
Capturing Cara (Dragon Lords of Valdier: Book 2)
Tracking Trisha (Dragon Lords of Valdier: Book 3)
Ambushing Ariel (Dragon Lords of Valdier: Book 4)
Cornering Carmen (Dragon Lords of Valdier: Book 5)
Paul's Pursuit (Dragon Lords of Valdier: Book 6)
Twin Dragons (Dragon Lords of Valdier: Book 7)

Lords of Kassis Series
River's Run (Lords of Kassis: Book 1)
Star's Storm (Lords of Kassis: Book 2)
Jo's Journey (Lords of Kassis: Book 3)
Ristéard's Unwilling Empress (Lords of Kassis: Book 4)

Magic, New Mexico Series
Touch of Frost (Magic, New Mexico Book 1)
Taking on Tory (Magic, New Mexico Book 2)

Sarafin Warriors
Choosing Riley (Sarafin Warriors: Book 1)

Viper's Defiant Mate (Sarafin Warriors Book 2)
The Alliance Series
Hunter's Claim (The Alliance: Book 1)
Razor's Traitorous Heart (The Alliance: Book 2)
Dagger's Hope (The Alliance: Book 3)
Zion Warriors Series
Gracie's Touch (Zion Warriors: Book 1)
Krac's Firebrand (Zion Warriors: Book 2)

Paranormal and Time Travel Novels
Spirit Pass Series
Indiana Wild (Spirit Pass: Book 1)
Spirit Warrior (Spirit Pass Book 2)
Second Chance Series
Lily's Cowboys (Second Chance: Book 1)
Touching Rune (Second Chance: Book 2)

Young Adult Novels
Breaking Free Series
Voyage of the Defiance (Breaking Free: Book 1)

Recommended Reading Order Lists:
http://sesmithfl.com/reading-list-by-events/
http://sesmithfl.com/reading-list-by-series/

About S.E. Smith

S.E. Smith is a *New York Times, USA TODAY, International, and Award-Winning* Bestselling author of science fiction, fantasy, paranormal, and contemporary works for adults, young adults, and children. She enjoys writing a wide variety of genres that pull her readers into worlds that take them away.

CPSIA information can be obtained
at www.ICGtesting.com
Printed in the USA
LVOW04s1106260516

489632LV00018BB/181/P

9 781942 562566